"Don't run away."

Evie's breath caught in her throat. "I have to," she whispered.

"You act like I'm some sort of threat to you," he said, and rubbed the underside of her arm with his fingers. "I'm not. At least, not intentionally."

"That's not it. I'm a threat to myself," she admitted, hypnotized by his gentle caress. "I'm feeling so… I'm not sure what exactly. But I know I shouldn't be feeling whatever it is. Maybe that doesn't make sense—I don't know. I only know that you'll be gone in three weeks and I'll still be here. And I have to make sure I'll be here with myself and my life intact."

His touch continued to hold her captive. "I have no intention of taking advantage of you, Evie," he said softly, his voice as seductive as the soft stroke of his fingertips. "And if you feel like you've been suddenly hit by a freight train—well, frankly, so do I."

Dear Reader,

I'm so happy to welcome you back to Crystal Point and to my second Harlequin Special Edition novel, *Marriage Under the Mistletoe*.

You might remember Evie Dunn from *Made for Marriage*. Evie is a sensible, reliable woman who has no time in her life for romance. She's a widow and mother and the kind of person who makes a good friend. She's also the second eldest of her siblings and the person everyone goes to for advice.

When Scott Jones arrives in Crystal Point to attend his sister's wedding he quickly falls for Evie. However, she has no intention of falling in love with the young and sexy fireman. But it's Christmas and, well, there's mistletoe....

I loved writing this book because it made me think about family and the dynamic between siblings, sisters in particular, and how we each have a role to play in our own family unit. I hope you enjoy Evie and Scott's story and I invite you to return to Crystal Point very soon.

I love to hear from readers—I can be reached via my website at www.helenlacey.com.

Warmest wishes,

Helen Lacey

MARRIAGE UNDER THE MISTLETOE

HELEN LACEY

HARLEQUIN®

entertain, enrich, inspire™

Recycling programs
for this product may
not exist in your area.

ISBN-13: 978-0-373-65708-7

MARRIAGE UNDER THE MISTLETOE

Books by Helen Lacey

Harlequin Special Edition

Made for Marriage #2166
Marriage Under the Mistletoe #2226

HELEN LACEY

grew up reading *Black Beauty, Anne of Green Gables* and *Little House on the Prairie*. These childhood classics inspired her to write her first book when she was seven years old, a story about a girl and her horse. She continued to write, with the dream of one day being a published author, and writing for Harlequin Special Edition is the realization of that dream. She loves creating stories about strong heroes with a soft heart and heroines who get their happily-ever-after. For more about Helen, visit her website, www.helenlacey.com.

For Jacqueline
Who told me there was no Santa, who always said I was
adopted and whose old clothes never really fit me right.
Because sisters really do make the best friends.

Chapter One

Evie Dunn pushed her feet from under the uncomfortable airport seat and let out a long sigh. Two hours of waiting in the arrivals terminal had stretched her patience. And she'd never liked airports all that much. There were too many people leaving, too many sad faces, too many goodbyes.

She looked at the cardboard sign in her hand and traced the outline of letters with her forefinger. Her soon-to-be sister-in-law's kid brother was on the twelve o'clock out of Los Angeles via Sydney, and she'd agreed to pick him up. Because that's what Evie did. She picked up, she dropped off. Rock-solid Evie. Ever-reliable Evie.

Boring-as-oatmeal Evie.

Not true. She made the correction immediately. She *wasn't* boring. She was dependable and responsible. Nothing wrong with that. Nothing at all. And today she was acting true to form after agreeing to make the four-hour road trip from Crystal Point to Brisbane and back again.

If Evie's nephew hadn't fallen from his bike and broke his arm, Callie would have been doing this. *I wish Callie was here now.*

She liked who she was. Most of the time. When the twinges came—those niggling little voices telling her to break out, to take a risk, to be wild and unpredictable for once in her life—she pushed them back to where they belonged. Which was not in her world. She had a business to run and a teenage son to raise. Taking risks wasn't on her horizon.

Passengers filed out of the gate, some greeting friends and family, some walked on alone. Evie stood up and held the sign out in front of her. As the parade of people dwindled, a tall, brown-haired man caught her attention. He moved with a confident lope, as though he was in no hurry, like a man with all the time in the world. And he looked a little familiar. Were they the same blue eyes as Callie's? He wore khaki cargo pants belted low on his hips, a black T-shirt and he had an army-style duffel bag flung over one shoulder. He was broad, toned and gorgeous.

This is no kid brother.

His pace slowed and his eyes scanned the crowd, clearly looking for someone. He met her eyes. He looked at the sign, then Evie, then back to the sign. Seconds later he smiled. A killer smile that radiated through to the soles of her feet. He stopped a couple of meters in front of her and looked her over. A long, leisurely look that made her toes curl. For one ridiculous moment she wished she'd paid more attention to her appearance that morning.

"Hey, I guess you're my ride?"

The soft, deeply resonant American drawl struck her low in the belly. She stuck out her hand. "Hi," she said, aware her voice sounded unusually high pitched. "I'm Evie—Noah's sister."

His hand was big and easily wrapped around hers. "Scott," he said. "Nice to meet you."

Scott Jones aka The Most Gorgeous Man She Had Ever Laid Eyes On.

And about a generation too young for a thirty-six-year-old woman.

She cleaved her dry tongue from the roof of her mouth. "Did you have a good flight?"

"Reasonable. I had a three-hour stopover in Sydney after getting through customs."

Evie ignored the rapid pump of her heart behind her ribs. "You can sleep some on the drive back if you like."

He shrugged lightly. "I appreciate the lift."

"No problem."

"I guess I should collect my luggage."

She nodded. "Sure. But first I think I should see your identification?"

"Huh?"

Evie squared her shoulders. "I need to make sure you're who you say you are," she said, ever cautious, always responsible.

He smiled and exposed the most amazing dimple in his cheek. "Okay," he said, and reached into his back pocket.

Evie didn't miss the way his biceps flexed as he moved. He pulled his passport out and handed it to her. She read his name—Scott Augustus Jones—and wasn't surprised to see he was photogenic, too. Evie returned the document to him.

He smiled again. "Do you want to frisk me now?"

Evie nearly burst a blood vessel. "I don't...I don't think so," she spluttered, feeling embarrassed and foolish. He was joking, of course. However, out of nowhere came the idea of running her hands across that chest and those thighs, and it made her hot all over. "Let's go to baggage claim."

He continued to smile and followed her down the escalators and she became increasingly aware of him behind her. And mindful of how dowdy and plain she must look to him in her faded denim skirt and biscuit-colored blouse. She smoothed her hands down her hips and tilted her chin.

It took about three minutes to find his bag and another five to reach her car. She was glad she'd borrowed her brother's dual-cab utility vehicle instead of driving her own small sedan. She couldn't imagine Scott Jones spending lengthy hours cramped up in her zippy Honda. Not with those long, powerful legs, broad shoulders, strong arms...

She sucked in a breath. *Get a grip. And fast.*

It had been forever since she'd really thought about a man in such a way. Oh, there'd been the odd inkling or an occasional vague and random thought. Mostly memories of the husband she'd loved and lost. But that was all. Acting on those thoughts was out of the question. She was a widow and mother, after all.

Ten years. The words swirled around in her head. An entire decade of abstinence. *That would almost give me a free pass into a convent.*

She looked at him again, as briefly as she could without appearing obvious.

Young came to mind immediately. *And Callie's brother. And only here for three weeks. And not my type.*

Gordon had been her type. Strong and sensible. Her first and only love. They'd been happy together. But dealing with his senseless death had been hard. After that, she buried herself along with her husband. Buried the part of her that screamed *woman* and got on with living.

Or so she thought.

"Thank you for the ride."

Evie didn't budge her eyes and drove from the car park. "You said that already."

He shifted in his seat and stretched his legs. "So, what happened to the kid?"

"Matthew fell off his bike two days ago and broke his arm. He's out of hospital, but Callie didn't want to leave him."

Evie admired her brother's fiancée. Callie had embraced her role as mother to Noah's four children and had quickly become the tonic the family needed. When four-year-old Matthew had his accident, Evie had quickly stepped in to taxi Callie's brother from Brisbane to Crystal Point. With her wedding only weeks away, the home she was selling in the middle of renovations and Matthew needing attention, Callie had enough on her plate without having to worry about her younger brother being stranded at the airport.

Only, Evie hadn't expected him to look like *this*.

And she hadn't expected her skin to feel just that little bit more alive, or her breath to sound as if it couldn't quite get out of her throat quick enough. *Okay, so that only proves that I still have a pulse.*

"So," she said, way more cheerfully than she felt, "what do you do for a living?"

He looked sideways. "I work for the Los Angeles Fire Department."

Evie's heart stilled. A firefighter? A hazardous occupation. Exactly what she needed to throw a bucket of cold water over her resurfacing libido. "That's a dangerous job?"

"It can be."

Evie's curiosity soared. *Ask the question.* "So why do you do it?"

"Someone has to, don't you think?"

"I guess." He had a point. But it didn't stop her thinking about the risks. She'd had years of practice thinking about risks, about dangers. A decade of thinking. Since the rainy night Gordon had donned his Volunteer Emergency Services jacket and left her with the promise to return, but never did. An awful night long ago. The night she'd shut down. She wondered about Scott's motives. "But why do *you* do it? Are you an adrenaline junkie?"

He chuckled. It was such an incredibly sexy sound that Evie's cheeks flamed.

"I'm sure my mom and sister think so."

"But you don't?"

"I do it because it's my job. Because it's what I'm trained to do. I don't think about the reasons why. Do you sit down and analyze why you're doing what you do?"

No. Because a shut-down person didn't question herself. A shut-down person was all about control, the now. But she didn't admit that. It was better to sound like everyone else. "Sometimes."

"What exactly do you do?"

"I run a bed-and-breakfast."

He nodded. "Yeah, I think Callie told me that. And you've got a kid?"

"Trevor," she replied. "He's fifteen."

Although she remained focused on the road, Evie felt his surprised stare.

"You must have married young."

Evie pushed her hair from her face. "By some standards, I suppose. I was nineteen."

She could almost hear him do the math in his head and felt about one hundred years old. While he, she knew, was just twenty-seven.

She pushed the CD button on, waited for music to fill the cab and resisted the urge to sing along.

"Do you want to share the driving?"

Evie looked sideways. "We drive on the other side of the road."

"I have an international license."

Of course he did. He was young, gorgeous, fearless and accomplished. "I'll let you know."

He didn't say anything for a while and relief pitched in her chest, although she felt the nearness of him through to her blood. What was it about men who looked like Scott Jones that made some women discard their usual good sense and want to jump their bones? But not her. Evie wasn't about to make a fool of herself over a great body and an incredible smile.

She cast a quick look in his direction. His eyes were shut. Good. If he slept she wouldn't have to talk. Besides, they had three weeks to get through, including the wedding, Christmas and New Year's.

And she could bet, right down to the soles of her feet, that they'd turn out to be three of the longest weeks in history.

Scott wanted to sleep. He longed for it. But he couldn't remember the last time he'd caught more than a couple of hours without being bombarded by dreams.

Yes, I can...

Eight months, he thought. *Give or take a day.* It had been eight months since his colleague and friend Mike O'Shea had been killed. And he'd lived under a cloud of guilt and blame and regret ever since.

Because despite being acquitted of any negligence involving the incident that had taken Mike's life, Scott *felt* responsible. He *should* have been able to save his friend. He should have tried harder, moved faster, relied on instinct rather than adhering to protocol. Mike had deserved that. So did the two young daughters and grieving wife he'd left behind.

It proved to Scott that a man with his profession couldn't have it all. The job he had, the job he loved…that job and family didn't mix. The wife-and-kids kind of family that meant commitment on a big scale. He'd been in love once, a few years back. He'd thought being involved with another firefighter would work, that she would understand the job, the pressures and the dangers involved. It lasted eighteen months before she'd bailed on him, their apartment and their plans for a future.

He should have expected it. Love hadn't figured in his life since. Lust…well, that was different. Since Belinda had walked out he'd dated half a dozen different women. He'd slept with a few of them but had no inclination to pursue anything serious. Because serious wasn't for him. Not while he was a firefighter.

Scott inhaled a deep breath and got a whiff of perfume. Something sweet…vanilla. He smiled when his brain registered how much he liked it. The woman beside him was extremely attractive; although she was so uptight he could feel the vibrations coming off her skin. But he liked the way she looked. He'd always been a sucker for long, dark, sexy hair. She had a nice mouth and big green eyes beneath slanting, provocative eyebrows. The type of woman he'd notice. *Lush,* he thought. And touchable in a way that could make a man's palms itch.

Maybe I should talk to her and break the ice a bit? Talking with women had never been a problem. He liked women. They usually liked him. But she didn't seem interested in conversation, so Scott kept his eyes closed and concentrated on the soft music beating between them.

Sleep…yeah…I can do that.

* * *

Evie had a headache. Probably from the tightly clenched jaw she couldn't relax. Acutely conscious of the sleeping man beside her, she gripped the wheel and looked directly ahead. An hour and a half into the journey and she felt the need to stop for a fix of caffeine. She pulled into a truck stop twenty minutes later and maneuvered the pickup into a vacant space outside the diner. Her passenger didn't stir as she turned off the engine and unclipped her belt. She looked him over and experienced a strange dip low in her belly. Really low.

Okay....so my body's not quite the museum I thought it was.

Evie wasn't sure how this sudden attraction made her feel. She wasn't sure she wanted to *feel* anything. She wasn't sure she even knew how anymore. Oh, she knew how to love her son, and her parents and her siblings and her nieces and nephews. And she was a good, loyal friend.

But a man? A flesh-and-blood man like the one in front of her—that was a different kind of *feeling* altogether. Memories of those kinds of feelings swam around in her head, like ghosts of a life once lived, a life that belonged to someone else.

The life of a woman who'd had a husband, a lover, a soul mate. When Gordon was alive she'd had those things. They'd laughed and loved. She felt passion and heat and sweat.

But Evie wasn't that woman anymore.

She took a breath, grabbed her purse and got out as quietly as she could. The restaurant wasn't busy and she quickly ordered coffee to go and a couple of prepackaged sandwiches. Evie hung around the counter until the order came, then stopped to collect sugar and plastic spoons from a small table near the door. She was just about to pocket some of both when she heard a voice behind her.

"How's the coffee here?"

She turned. Scott was close. Really close. His chest seemed like a solid wall in front of her. "I'm not sure." She held up a small cardboard carrier containing two foam cups. "It's hot at least."

"That's a good start."

Evie's skin prickled. "I wasn't sure how you liked it."

He smiled. "Black, two sugars and milk."

A funny guy. Great. She passed him four sachets of sugar. "Knock yourself out."

"Shall we sit?" he asked.

Evie handed over the coffee. "Sure."

She grabbed the food and followed him to one of the melamine tables and contained her surprise when he pulled out a chair for her. "How much do I owe you?" he asked once seated.

Evie shook her head and flouted the way her heart pounded beneath her ribs like a freight train. "My treat."

He smiled again and she got another look at the dimple. "Thanks." He took the lid off his coffee and poured in some sugar. "Callie tells me you're in the wedding party?" he asked, resting both elbows on the table.

She nodded and pushed a sandwich toward him. "And you're giving the bride away?"

"Yeah." He looked at her over the rim of his cup. "So, what else do you do besides run a B and B?"

Evie carefully sipped her coffee. "I paint."

"Houses?"

"Pictures," she replied. "Portraits, landscapes…that sort of thing."

"Talented *and* beautiful," he said smoothly.

Color rose up her collarbone and she felt like shaking

her head to refute the compliment. Evie knew she *wasn't* beautiful. She had even enough features and was attractive at best. Her sister Grace, on the other hand, was a classic beauty. And Mary-Jayne, the youngest of the three sisters, had always been considered the pretty one. Evie was just…Evie.

"And I teach art classes at my studio. What about you?" she asked, ignoring the compliment. "What do you do?"

"Besides what I'm doing now?" he replied, then shrugged. "The usual, I suppose."

"The usual?" she echoed.

He put down his cup and leaned back in the chair. "I work."

Evie took a breath. *Talk. Say something. I talk to people every day. I'm good at talking.* "And when do you play?"

It wasn't exactly what she'd planned to say. Because it sounded outright flirtatious. And she *never* flirted. Without warning, the sexy-as-sin Scott Jones had somehow tapped in to the female part of her she'd kept under wraps for a decade.

"I mean," she said quickly, covering her escalating embarrassment. "Do you like sports and stuff?"

"I like sports." He smiled. "Do you?"

"I like to *watch* sports," she admitted. "Even the macho sweaty kind like football."

"But you don't play?"

She shrugged, suddenly feeling like a couch potato. "I run."

"Me, too."

With that body he did more than run—Evie would bet her boots on it.

"Shall we get going?" she asked, changing the subject. Before he had a chance to reply she grabbed her coffee and food and made her way outside. The late-afternoon sun was settling toward dusk and they still had another three hours driving ahead. It would be well after dark by the time they arrived into Crystal Point.

She hopped into the driver's seat, started the engine and waited until they were both buckled up before heading off. They had a few minutes of silence before he spoke.

"Lacrosse."

Evie slanted a sideways look. "What?"

"You'd probably like it," he said. "It can be macho and sweaty."

"I thought it was badminton on steroids?"

He laughed, and the sound thrilled her down to her toes. "*Ouch.* You don't miss a man's ego with that aim."

A smile curled the edges of her mouth. "I'm guessing you play?"

"Yes. I still think you'd like it."

"The next time I'm in L.A. I'll be sure to catch a game."

"Have you ever been?"

"Once," she replied. "Years ago. Gordon and I did the whole tourist thing just after we were married."

"Gordon? That was your husband?"

"Yes, he was." Her voice automatically softened. "He's dead."

"Callie told me that," he said soberly. "You must miss him."

"Yes."

"Were you happy?"

She shot a glance sideways for a moment. It was a highly personal question from a stranger. *A stranger who would soon be family. Part of the Preston clan.* Except, she hadn't been Evie Preston for a long time. She was Evie Dunn, mother of one—*mother-hen,* her father often called her. The girl most likely to fade into the background and do whatever needed to be done. The sensible daughter.

"We were very happy," she said quietly.

"And does your son look like his father?"

"No," she replied. "Trevor looks like me."

"Lucky kid."

Another compliment. He was good at them. He had an easygoing way about him and a kind of masculine confidence she figured he'd probably possessed since the cradle.

Evie was tempted to say thank you, but she caught herself before the words left her mouth.

He stretched out his legs and she couldn't stop herself from glancing at his thighs.

I really need to pull myself together...and fast.

She went for a rabbit in a hat. "So, your girlfriend couldn't come on this trip with you?"

"I'm single," he replied flatly.

"Sorry," she said automatically. "I didn't mean to pry."

He looked at her again. She felt the burning intensity of his gaze through to her blood. He wasn't fooled, either. She *wanted* to know, foolishly, if there was a woman in his life. And she felt stupid. Incredibly stupid. Like a silly teenager gushing over the new boy in school.

She glanced at him, hoping he didn't notice, and wondered where all these sudden hormones had come from. Okay, so he wasn't a boy. He was the furthest thing from a boy.

But he's young. Way younger than acceptable.

Boy-Toy sprang to mind. Ridiculous. *Cougar* followed on its tail, racing around in her head like a chant, telling her to stop dreaming impossible dreams.

"I broke up with my ex-girlfriend over a year ago."

Evie looked at Scott again, slanting her gaze sideways while concentrating on the road ahead. "I'm sorry."

"Are you?"

She gripped the steering wheel. "I guess…" Her words

trailed, then stopped. "Actually I'm usually not one for platitudes. So I'll happily take that back and stop sticking my nose where it doesn't belong."

"It would be a shame to waste such a pretty nose, don't you think?"

Evie's skin tingled. He turned a good line. She pointed to a stack of CDs in the center console. "You can choose some music if you like."

He took a moment before flicking through the pile, and then Jack Johnson's voice filtered through the cab.

"Good pick," she said on a sharp breath.

"You sound surprised?"

Evie stared directly ahead. "My son tossed them to me this morning. I had no idea what he'd chosen. I expected—"

"That I'd go for something a little less mellow?"

"I guess."

"I was raised on a steady diet of jazz from my father, and classic bands like The Eagles and Bread from my mom, who was, and still is a seventies purist," he explained. "I like most types of music."

Evie felt distinctly put in her place. "Sorry."

"That's a favorite word of yours."

Around you it is. But she didn't say it. All she wanted to do was stop thinking about his washboard belly, unfairly cute dimple and nice voice.

"I'll just…" she began, and then stalled because she knew he was looking at her, summing her up and working her out. "I'm really quite okay to not talk if you'd prefer. You've had a long flight and I'm…"

He laughed softly. "Chill out, Evie," he said with a grin she couldn't see but knew was on his lips. "I can cope without conversation."

He settled back in the seat and Evie drew in a sharp breath, feeling like such a fraud. She wasn't sure why. She wasn't sure she wanted to know why. She only knew that in a matter of hours, her life—the life she'd lived for so many years—seemed a lot like a life half-lived.

It was as though she'd been asleep for years, not thinking, not wondering. But Evie was wondering now. And she was awake. *Wide* awake.

Chapter Two

Scott woke up in a strange bed. He rolled onto his back, blinked twice and took stock of his surroundings. A nice room with sloping walls. A comfortable mattress. Clean sheets that smelled like fresh-squeezed lemons. Another scent caught his attention. Coffee. And vanilla.

Green eyes, lips the color of ripe California cherries, dark curly hair dancing down a woman's back.

Evie Dunn.

Scott quickly remembered where he was. *I'm in Evie's bed.*

Well, not technically *her* bed. Although that idea unexpectedly appealed to him when he inhaled another whiff of coffee laced with vanilla. A bed in her house. And not in the B and B part of the big home. These were her private quarters. That had surprised him. But she'd explained how the rooms were fully booked over the holiday season and with Callie and Noah's wedding organized so suddenly she hadn't time enough to change her bookings.

He checked the clock on the bedside table. Six o'clock. He'd been asleep for over nine hours. When they'd arrived at Dunn Inn the night before, he'd pretty much crashed within half an hour of dumping his duffel at the end of the bed.

Scott's stomach growled. He was hungry. And his body ached. He swung out of bed and planted his feet on the floorboards. *I need a run.* He stood, stretched and then rummaged through his bag for sweats. *It's summer here, remember?* He opted instead for shorts and a T-shirt, pulled on socks and trainers, found his iPod and left the room.

He headed down the hall and took the flight of stairs. The rich scent of coffee hit him again as he got to the side door and the private entrance Evie told him he could use. He could hear voices coming from the guest area and main kitchen and fought the urge to follow the sound. She was obviously busy. But he looked forward to seeing those sparkling green eyes again.

Once outside, Scott got a good look at the house. It was huge and had long windows protected by timber shutters and a gabled roof. He walked backward out of the front yard to the garden. Then he turned and was struck by the most incredible view of the Pacific Ocean barely one hundred meters away. As kids he and Callie had vacationed in the nearby town of Bellandale a few times, where their father had been born. But Scott had never seen Crystal Point before. Callie had told him about it, of course, and he'd listened to his sister's stories about small-town life and the camaraderie among the residents and how she'd been readily accepted by the community. And Scott knew her marriage to Noah Preston would cement that bond and she'd never return to California.

He looked toward the ocean, inhaling deeply. The sea was as flat as glass and he spotted a couple of fishing boats on the horizon. He liked this place. Especially when he looked to his left and spotted Evie Dunn pounding the pavement on incredibly athletic legs. She jogged toward him, zigzagging across a wide stretch of grass between the road and the footpath. Black shorts flipped across her thighs as she moved. She wore a white tank shirt, bright pink socks and flashy new trainers, and her glorious hair was pulled back and tied up beneath an equally pink visor. Scott swallowed hard. She looked vibrant and wholly desirable.

"Hey," she said, coming to a halt about six feet in front of him. "I didn't think you'd be up this early." She took in big gulps of air and planted her hands on her hips.

"I told you I run," he said, trying not to look as though he was checking her out. He managed a smile and kept his gaze level with hers. "Perhaps next time we could go together?"

"Perhaps," she said. "Well, I'd better go inside. I've got hungry guests waiting."

She smiled and headed off past him at a slow jog. Scott turned instinctively and watched her until she disappeared around the side of the house. He liked the way she moved. He liked her curvy, athletic body.

A jolt of attraction ran through him, stronger this time. Not what he wanted. *Definitely* not. She wasn't the casual kind of woman like those he'd been seeing since he'd broke up with Belinda. Evie Dunn looked like the kind of woman who'd want permanence—and more than that—she looked like the kind of woman who'd *need* permanence.

And that's not me.

Commitment had no place in his life. He had his job—a job he had to prove to himself that he could do without distraction.

He put the earbuds in place and turned up the volume on the iPod. Stretching his travel-weary muscles for a few minutes, he then went for a long run and decided not to think about Evie's great legs, or lovely hips or bright green eyes. He would just have to forget all about her.

The Manning sisters had been coming to Dunn Inn for nine years. Both in their seventies, both widows who'd married twin brothers, they shared a profound camaraderie that Evie knew she'd have with her own sisters throughout the years. Her sisters were her best friends, her confidantes, her conscience, her troubleshooters. She wondered what they would think of her new houseguest—or the semierotic dream she'd had about him the night before.

Evie listened to Flora Manning explain her newest recipe for double chocolate fudge brownies while she served them breakfast in the main dining room. Sticklers for tradition, the sisters preferred to have all their meals in the bigger room, and forgo Evie's usual and more casual approach of breakfast in the kitchen. Most of her guests favored that particular meal at the long wooden table where they could chat among themselves and with Evie.

But the Manning sisters liked the good china and the pressed tablecloths and the fresh flowers Evie always maintained in the formal dining area. And because her next guests weren't arriving until that afternoon, Evie gave Flora and Amelia a little extra attention.

"Did we see you talking with a man outside?" Amelia asked as she sipped her tea.

Evie looked up from her spot at the buffet table. There was clearly nothing wrong with the Manning sisters' eyesight despite their recent protestations about their failing senses. "He's here for my brother's wedding."

"Ah," Flora said, nodding to her sister. "Told you so."

"Mmm," she replied, and placed a rack of toast and petite pots of marmalade on a serving plate.

"He's a nice-looking young man," Amelia said.

Definitely nothing wrong with their eyesight. "I guess he is."

"And he's staying until after the wedding?" Amelia asked.

Evie nodded. "Up until New Year's, I believe."

The sisters shared another look. "Is he a relative of yours?"

"No," she replied. "He's Callie's brother. As you know, Callie's engaged to my brother."

Two sets of silver eyebrows rose. "Is he married?"

"No."

Another look—this one a little triumphant. "Straight?" Flora, the more to-the-point sister, asked.

Evie smiled to herself. "Yes."

"You should find yourself a man." Flora again, never one to hold back, spoke as she smoothed out her perfectly groomed chignon. "Your son needs a father."

Heat prickled up her spine. "He has a father."

Flora tutted. "A ghost," she said. "The same ghost you cling to."

Evie's hands stilled. "Not a ghost," she said, probably a little sharper than she would have liked. But she knew the sisters' cared about her. Telling it how they saw it was simply their way. "Just memories of a good man."

"Just promise you'll think about it," Amelia said with a soft smile. "Now, when are you going to finish decorating the house?"

Good question. With Christmas only weeks away Evie

usually had all the trimmings up. Granted, the beautiful cypress tree stood center stage in the living room and looked remarkable with its jewel-colored decorations and lights. Noah usually helped her with the rest of the garlands and tinsel she always scattered around the big house. But this year was different. He and Callie had their own home to decorate, and Evie hadn't wanted to bother her brother simply because she wasn't tall enough to finish decking the halls.

"I'll get to it as soon as I can," she promised, thinking the ladder in the shed out back would do the trick.

She returned to the main kitchen and left the sisters with their breakfast. She was just stacking the dishwasher when the door connecting the guest quarters and the stairwell leading to her private residence opened. Her sleepy-looking son emerged.

"Good morning," she greeted.

"We're out of milk upstairs," he muttered, eyes half-closed.

Evie opened the refrigerator and took out a plastic carton of milk for her cereal-addicted son. "Try and make it last past this afternoon," she teased.

"Sure," he said. "Hey, can I have twenty bucks? There's a computer gaming party at Cody's tomorrow night and we all want to pitch in for snacks."

Evie raised one brow. "What happened to your allowance this week?"

He shrugged. "I could say the dog ate it."

"We don't have a dog."

"But we should get one," Trevor said, swiftly employing his usual diversion tactics as he draped one arm across her shoulders and grinned. "It could be a guard dog. Especially for those times when I'm not here and you're all alone."

"I'm rarely alone," Evie said. "We have a seventy-five-percent occupancy rate, remember?"

"I remember. So, about that twenty bucks?"

"If you help me put up the rest of the Christmas decorations tonight, I'll consider it."

Trevor rolled his eyes. "Well, I have to—"

"No help, no snack money."

Her son's dark hair flopped across his forehead. "Okay," he agreed begrudgingly. "But I'm not wearing a Santa hat while I do it like you made me last year."

"Spoilsport." She checked her watch. "You better go upstairs and finish breakfast. Cody's mother will be here soon to drive you to school." She took a few strides toward him and gave his cheek a swift kiss. "And don't forget the milk."

As one young male raced out of the room, another walked right on in through the back door. Only *this* young man set her pulse soaring. It should be illegal for any man to have arms like that. The pale blue T-shirt did little to disguise the solid muscle definition. She spotted a Celtic braid tattoo banding his right biceps. *Oh, sweet heaven.*

Scott smiled when he saw where he'd ended up. "I think I took the wrong door."

Evie managed not to look him over as if he were a very tasty hot lunch. He looked as though he'd been running hard. His hair, a kind of dark hazelnut color, stuck to his forehead in parts while sweat trickled down his collarbone.

"You should find yourself a man."

Flora Manning's words returned with vengeance. Should she? Was that what she wanted? Sure—Evie was attracted to him. Any woman would be, right? He was young and gorgeous and had somehow kick-started her sleeping sexuality. But it was just *lust.* Just attraction. And attraction was…well, pointless if it wasn't backed up with something more, wasn't it? With Gordon she'd had more. She'd had love and loyalty. *A marriage.* Happiness.

Evie swallowed. "It's a big house. You'll get the hang of it."

"I don't remember much of the tour you gave me last night, I'm afraid," he said, just a little breathless.

"Did you sleep okay?"

He nodded and took in a few gulps of air. "Like a baby."

Evie had a startling image in her head of long, power-ful legs and smooth silk-on-steel skin wrapped in cotton bedsheets. She cleared her throat in an effort to stop her thoughts from wandering any further. "Breakfast will be upstairs."

"You're joining me?"

"Er—yes. I just have to see to my guests." She quickly explained about the Manning sisters.

"I'll see you upstairs, then," he said, and chose that moment to grab the hem of his T-shirt and wipe the sweat from his face. Evie's eyes almost popped out of her head as she caught sight of the most amazing abs she'd ever seen. A six-pack. *A twelve-pack.* She could swear he'd heard the rush of breath from her lips and felt the vibration of her heart pounding like an out-of-control jackhammer.

"Yeah…okay."

He disappeared through the door that led upstairs, and it wasn't until she heard his footsteps on the top of the landing that she left the kitchen and returned to the din-ing room. The sisters were still sipping tea and peeling the crusts off toast, and Evie collected a few dishes and told them she'd be back later for the rest. When she was done in the main kitchen, she headed upstairs. She could hear water running in the guest bathroom and relaxed fraction-ally. Trevor was placing his empty cereal bowl in the sink when she entered the kitchenette and pantry. They heard the familiar beep of a horn outside.

"That's my ride. I gotta go." Trevor grabbed his knapsack and left on fast feet.

Evie filled the jug and pulled two mugs from the cupboard. By the time Scott reappeared about ten minutes later, she'd chopped fruit and set the small table she usually only shared with her son.

Faded jeans fitted over his hips, and the black T-shirt did little to disguise the breadth of his broad shoulders and flat stomach. His feet were bare, his hair freshly washed. He smelled clean and extraordinarily masculine. The mood felt uncomfortably intimate and Evie suddenly regretted agreeing to allow him to stay in her home. Downstairs would have been better. Downstairs was about business. Upstairs was her private world. A world she shared with her son. A world no man had entered for ten years.

He looked around and then pulled out a chair. "This is an incredible house," he said easily. "You have good taste."

And I'll bet you taste good...

She cleared her throat and held up the jug. "Coffee?"

"For sure." He sat down. "Is there anything you'd like me to do?"

Desperate to change the subject, Evie grabbed a couple of slices of bread. "So, how do you like your toast?"

He smiled. "However you'd like to give it to me," he said, and looked at the bread flapping in her hands.

Evie did her best to ignore the inflammatory words and placed the bread in the toaster, set out two plates and grabbed the diced fruit. Once the toast popped and the jug boiled, she poured coffee and moved toward the small table.

"You didn't answer my question," he said, taking the

coffee she slid across the table. "About anything you need doing around the place while I'm living with you."

Evie felt the familiarity of his words down to her feet. She should have insisted he stay at her parents' house instead of volunteering to keep him at Dunn Inn. *Keep him?* She meant *have him.* No, that wasn't right, either. *I'm not having him. I'm not having anyone.*

"I've got it covered. Besides, you're on vacation, aren't you?" she asked as she placed the food on the table and shifted her thoughts from his fabulous abdominals to a more neutral topic.

"I guess," he replied, and placed toast on a plate. When she remained silent he looked up. "I'd like to earn my keep, though."

"You're a guest," she said quietly.

"And family," he said, and bit into a piece of toast. "We'll be in-laws soon enough."

Evie met his blue eyes head-on.

"So, family does stuff for one another, right?"

Ever cautious, Evie narrowed her gaze. "What did you have in mind?"

"You tell me," he said easily. "It's a big house—I imagine there are always things that need doing."

I need doing came to mind and color immediately rose over her cheeks. She wanted Sensible Evie to come back. She needed her to come back before she made a complete fool of herself. But Sensible Evie had deserted her. In her place was I Haven't Had Sex In Ten Years Evie, and she was suddenly a strong, undeniable force.

"I'll let you know," she said. "But like I said, I've got it covered."

"You don't like taking help from people?"

Evie sucked in a breath. "Sure I do," she said, lying

through her teeth. "But I'm well practiced at doing what needs to be done through both habit and necessity."

"So I'm not stepping on anyone's toes by being here?" he asked, watching her with such burning scrutiny she had to turn her eyes away.

Evie knew what the question meant, knew he'd probably wondered if she had a man in her life. "No. There's just me and my son."

"Hard to believe," he said quietly.

She returned her gaze to his immediately. "What? That I'm single or that I choose to be that way?"

He smiled. "That you're not beating them off with a stick."

"Who says I'm not?"

Evie tried to look casual, tried to make out as though her heart wasn't thumping stupidly behind her ribs. But it was. In fact, her entire body was thumping—like a runaway train, like a horse galloping out of control.

"I stand corrected."

He was smiling and that incredible dimple showed itself. Okay, so she wasn't exactly turning potential lovers away at the door. But she'd had a few offers over the years. None she'd pursued.

"Are you okay, Evie?"

No...but she wasn't about to tell Mr. Great Body And Gorgeous Dimple that she was hot and bothered because of him. "Perfectly."

But he wasn't fooled. And neither was she. Something hung between them. Something unsaid. She picked at the fruit in front of her to avoid saying anything else. Once breakfast was over he offered to wash up. Evie was about to refuse when she heard the downstairs door open and a familiar voice called her name.

"That's Callie," Evie said, and pushed out her chair.

Scott did the same and moments later the kitchen door opened and his sister entered the room.

Callie stood in the threshold and her gaze flicked over them. Evie felt the scrutiny through to her bones. The kitchen was small, cozy, intimate. Evie knew the other woman could feel the invisible current in the air as much as she could.

Callie quickly came into the room and flung herself at her brother in an affectionate hug. Noah wasn't far behind and once Evie returned the keys to his truck the two men shook hands, quickly summed each other up as men seemed to be able to do without even speaking and started a quiet conversation. Then Callie headed Evie off by the sink.

"I can't thank you enough," Callie said on a rush of breath. "I mean, for picking up my little brother."

Little brother? Sure. Evie was struck by the remarkable resemblance between the siblings. Her soon-to-be sister-in-law was quite beautiful and Evie knew how deeply Noah loved the spirited and passionate brunette.

"No thanks necessary," she said, and set the dishes on the draining board. "It's—"

"Family," Callie said. "Yeah, I know. But I still appreciate it. I can't believe all the connecting flights from Brisbane to Bellandale were booked up."

"There's the big air show on this weekend," Evie explained. "Every flying enthusiast from around the state travels here for it. Same thing happens each year." She grabbed her rubber gloves. "Are the kids at my parents'?"

"Yes. We dropped them off before we came over here." Callie leaned back against the melamine countertop. "Matthew's enjoying the cast on his arm. Crazy to think we're at the end of the school year already. But I'm so looking forward to Christmas."

Evie smiled. "You *are* getting married Christmas Eve."

"Self-indulgent, I know," Callie said with such a bliss-fully happy grin Evie felt a tiny stab of envy. "Speaking of all things wedding—you and Fiona have an appointment with the dressmaker next Thursday at ten o'clock."

"It's on my list," Evie replied. "Fiona called me a few days ago to confirm." Fiona Walsh was the other bridesmaid in the wedding party and a friend of both Callie and Evie. "I'll be there."

"And thanks so much for your help with the caterers," Callie said. "I can't believe we've managed to organize all this in a little over a month. You're a genius. And a good friend."

"It's a special day," Evie said, and grinned. "And I like planning things."

"Fortunately for me."

"It will be a perfect evening," she assured her, sensing a few bride-to-be nerves in the usually composed Callie. "My brother's a lucky man."

Callie smiled dreamily. "I'm the lucky one."

The stab of envy returned and Evie squashed it down in a hurry. She wouldn't begrudge Callie her happiness. "You're both lucky. So are the kids."

Her friend looked radiant. *Have I ever looked like that? Yes, of course. Absolutely. Without a doubt.*

She'd loved Gordon since she was seventeen years old. He'd been her first kiss, first lover…her only lover. They'd shared dreams, values and the joy of raising their young son. And something else, a bond between two people so in tune with each other's thoughts, so completely at ease with each other it was as if they were halves of the same whole. And Evie didn't expect to ever have that again. And she wasn't about to throw herself out there looking for it.

Evie settled her gaze on Scott again, and her pulse

quickened. *It's just physical*. But despite the warning bells going off in her head, the attraction she felt for him suddenly poleaxed her.

Sex clouded judgments, right? Sex made people do crazy things. Inappropriate things. She had no illusions. Fantasies about a man nine years her junior were completely off the Richter scale in the good-sense department. Of course he wouldn't be interested in her. He'd have his pick. And he certainly wouldn't choose a thirty-six-year-old single mother well past her prime.

Besides, he was a firefighter. And men with dangerous occupations had no place in her life. She'd already lost one man to the elements. She wasn't about to start fantasizing about a man who chose to run into burning buildings.

That settled, Evie announced she had a B and B to run and excused herself. She was quietly relieved when Scott arranged to leave with his sister and Noah. She told him she'd left a spare key on the armoire in the guest bedroom and said goodbye to her brother and Callie before returning downstairs.

She had a lot of work to do. And a gorgeous man she had to get out of her head. Somehow.

Chapter Three

Scott spent most of the day with his sister. Callie's property, Sandhills Farm, was a few minutes out of Crystal Point. The For Sale sign out front was new and Callie explained how she had plans to relocate her horse riding school to Noah's larger property within the coming months.

"It's a big move," she said as they walked up through the stables. "But I've only ten acres here and I can easily take about twenty acres at Noah's. Plus, I don't want to be commuting every day and I want my horses close to me. I'm working on the house renovations now and will try to find a tenant if it doesn't sell quickly."

Scott didn't think she'd have a problem finding a buyer. Sandhills Farm was an impressive setup for any equestrian enthusiast, with its stable complex, round yards and sand arena. "So, you're happy?"

Callie's eyes opened wide. "Blissfully," she replied.

"Noah's just so…" She stopped, smiled a silly sort of smile Scott couldn't remember ever seeing on his sister's face before and let out a long sigh. "He's *everything*."

Everything? That was a tall order. Scott couldn't imagine being *everything* to any woman. Not even Belinda way back when he'd been convinced he was in love with her.

"I'm glad he makes you happy." *He'd better,* were the words unsaid.

Callie looped her arm through his. "What about you?" she asked. "Anyone special in your life at the moment?"

"No," he replied, thinking about Evie all of a sudden. He pushed the thought back quickly.

Callie smiled. "Are you looking?"

Scott raised both brows. "Not intentionally."

His sister gave him an odd look. "I wish you were staying longer," she said. "With Mom arriving in two weeks and the wedding just around the corner, I don't think I'll be much in the way of a tour guide while you're here."

Scott shrugged and looked around. "Don't worry about it. You've got more important things to think about."

Callie squeezed his forearm. "Well, I'm glad you're here. And you're in good hands with Evie."

Scott's stomach did a wild leap. Thinking about Evie Dunn's hands made him remember how she'd looked in her small kitchen earlier that morning. She'd looked… *beddable.* Was there such a word? In jeans and a white loose-fitting shirt that exposed just enough of her collarbone to raise his temperature a degree or two, Scott had barely been able to drag his gaze away from her. She had lovely skin. And that hair—masses of dark curls reaching way past her shoulders. He'd wanted to twist it around his hands, tilt her head back and kiss the smooth skin along her throat.

"Scott, about Evie…"

He shifted on his feet. Had Callie read his thoughts? "What about her?"

She smiled fractionally. "She's, you know, my friend. And Noah's sister."

"The point being?"

Callie expelled a breath. "The point being that she's *my friend.* And there seemed to be a fair bit of heat between you in the kitchen this morning."

"You're imagining things." His sister raised both brows again and gave him a *look.* Scott held up a hand. "I left chasing everything in a skirt behind in my teens."

Callie gave a grim smile. "I know that. But since you and Belinda broke up and then Mike's death, you've changed and I—"

"Belinda was a long time ago," he said, cutting her off. "And I don't see what Mike has to do with any of this."

Callie shrugged. "He was your friend."

"And?"

"And losing a friend like that must be hard. And Evie, well, she's like a magnet. Everyone feels it about her. She's warm and generous and so incredibly likable. Anyone who meets her gets drawn in. I would hate to see her get hurt."

"By me?" Scott pushed back the irritation weaving up his back. Callie was way off base. Sure, he was attracted to Evie Dunn. But he had no intention of acting on that attraction. He already worked out that Evie wasn't for him.

Okay...maybe I did flirt with her a bit this morning. But flirting is harmless. It won't go anywhere. I'll make sure of that.

"You're jumping to conclusions," he said to his sister. "We barely know each other."

Callie made a face. "I know what I saw."

"Just drop it, Callie."

She did, but the thought stuck with Scott for the rest

of the afternoon. By the time Callie dropped him off at Dunn Inn, it was past three o'clock. Evie's car was parked in the driveway and Scott was just fishing in his pocket for his key when he spotted a teenage boy shooting hoops near the studio out back. And shooting them pretty badly.

The youth stopped playing when Scott approached and spoke. "Hi."

Scott smiled and shook the teenager's hand as he introduced himself. Evie Dunn's son seemed like a nice kid. Of course, Evie's kid wouldn't be anything else.

"Wanna shoot?" Trevor asked, and tossed the ball to him. "It would be good to see the thing actually go in the hoop."

Scott laughed and swiftly dropped the ball into the basket. "You just need to work on your angle."

Trevor shrugged and smiled. "I'm not much of a sportsman. Take after my mother, I guess."

Scott remembered how Evie had looked that morning in her running gear. She certainly seemed to keep herself in great shape. "She's an artist," Scott said, and then felt foolish.

Trevor looked at him oddly, but continued to smile. "I guess. My dad was the sporty one."

"Mine, too," Scott replied, and passed the ball on.

The teenager grabbed the basketball, aimed, concentrated and shot it at the hoop. It missed and rebounded directly into Scott's hands. "My dad's dead."

Scott lobbed the ball back through the hoop once it bounced. "Mine, too."

Trevor grabbed the ball and took another shot. The ball curved around the edges of the hoop before dropping to the side. "Yeah…it sucks."

They continued to shoot hoops and talk for several minutes, until a taxi pulled up outside the house and two elderly women emerged. As they walked slowly up the driveway, Trevor groaned under his breath. The women approached on quickening feet and Scott watched their progress with a broad grin.

It took them precisely five seconds to persuade Scott to help them carry their bags from the footpath and into the house. Trevor smiled as if he'd been given a Get Out Of Jail Free card and went back to shooting hoops.

There were about a dozen shopping bags from various retail outlets, and Scott guessed the two women had spent the day scouting the stores in Bellandale. The perfectly groomed pair were obviously the Manning sisters who Evie had told him about on the long drive from the airport. They regarded him with such blatant curiosity it felt as if their two sets of eyes were burning a hole through his back as he walked up the half dozen steps and opened the front screen door while juggling the parcels.

Once they'd stepped over the threshold, Scott closed the door and followed them through the house. *Vanilla.* The scent hit him immediately. *Evie.*

The living room was large and immaculately presented, but it was the huge, ornately decorated Christmas tree that held his attention. It was a real tree—the kind he remembered from when he was young and his father was still alive. Memories banged around in his head. They'd go out together and find the perfect tree, strap it to the roof of his father's Volvo and make the trip home laughing, because they both knew his mother would insist on moving the tree around for hours before she finally settled on a spot to showcase her decorating efforts. And they laughed because, inevitably, the tree ended up in the same position every year.

Funny, he didn't think about those days much anymore. He tried not to think about how much he still missed his father. He'd been a good man, and a good dad. But reckless. And that recklessness had contributed to his death. A desk jockey by day, his father would pursue one adventure after another on the weekend. Sailing, skiing, climbing. Ultimately, it was the climbing that killed him. His death had galvanized something inside Scott. At eighteen he had been determined to join the fire department and approached the job responsibly. He didn't take risks. He followed the rules.

And those rules didn't include fantasizing about Evie Dunn.

A widow. A single mom.

Two very good reasons to keep his head.

The Manning sisters thanked him for his help, and Scott was just about to make a quick exit when Evie walked into the room. She smiled at him and his chest tightened unexpectedly. He smiled back, saw her cheeks flush and then quickly she diverted her gaze. His thoughts lingered on how pretty she was. *And all that incredible, seriously sexy hair.* She started talking with the sisters, but he could feel the vibration of her awareness of him like a drum beating. Because she appeared to be trying *not* to look at him.

Scott had placed the bags near the foot of one of the sofas, and Evie and the elderly sisters began unloading the contraband. He stood back and watched, amused by the clear delight the three women displayed as bags were opened and items unwrapped. Evie's animated expression was addictive and he couldn't look away. He watched her unload parcels and sigh her appreciation for the treasures as she unwrapped close to a dozen shiny glass ornaments and garlands and laid them carefully on the sofa. Scott snatched a glance at the tree behind him and quickly realized something. *Evie loved Christmas.* He could easily imagine her trimming a turkey, wrapping gifts with matching paper and ribbon, singing carols on Christmas Eve and doing all the things that made the festive season special.

A magnet, Callie had called her. Someone who draws people in.

Was that what she was doing to him? But Scott was convinced it was just physical attraction. He'd been attracted to women before. Some he'd dated. Some he'd slept with.

Evie looked across at him briefly and the smile curling her lips made his stomach roll over. Her cheeks flushed again, brighter this time. Scott's fingers itched with the sudden urge to reach out and touch her face, to trace the line of her jaw and her delicious-looking mouth. Her lips parted, as if she knew he was thinking about them...wondering, imagining if they tasted as sweet as they looked. Her tongue came out and moistened her lower lip. The kick of it rushed to his feet, traveled up his legs and hit him square in the groin.

With his heart hammering behind his ribs, Scott looked at the two elderly women still fussing over their parcels and knew he had to get away from Evie...and fast. He cleared his throat and quickly excused himself.

By the time he'd returned to the private quarters and headed for his room, his breathing was back to normal. He sat on the edge of the big bed, took a deep breath and clenched his fists. *I'm not going to get involved here. I'm going home soon—back to my life—back to everything I know. Three weeks, Jones...I gotta keep it together.*

Evie lingered in the largest downstairs bedroom later that afternoon. She had guests arriving soon—a newly married couple who were staying for a week. The bedroom was her favorite in the house—big and airy and decorated in the palest hues of purple, lavender and white. It had its own bathroom and small sitting area, and the enormous bed was scattered with half a dozen cushions in various shades of mauve. She fluffed a couple of pillows, straightened the white lace bedspread and fiddled with the vase of lilac-and-cream miniature roses that sat on the dresser.

She thought about Scott. Her blood pumped when she remembered how he'd looked at her. The air had smoldered with a kind of throbbing, consuming, slowly building heat.

This is so crazy...he's twenty-seven years old, for heaven's sake.

Evie took a deep breath, straightened the already straight bedspread and headed upstairs. Back in her own room she looked out the window and saw her son shooting his basketball into the hoop. Scott was with him. They were talking and throwing the ball. She heard a shout of laughter from her son and it tightened something in her chest.

Oh...no...I'm not going to like him. But seeing him with her son made her like him. Not just lust, she thought, something else, an awareness of him on another level.

And Trevor's laughter made Evie ache inside. She knew her son longed for regular male company, a man's influence...a father's influence.

Imagining Scott in that role was foolish. He'd be gone in three weeks.

Her guests arrived about ten minutes later. In their mid-fifties and obviously in love, Trent and Patti Keller were all smiles when Evie showed them to their room. A tiny stab of envy knotted tightly and she tamped it down.

Evie gave them a tour of the house, and introduced them to the Manning sisters, who were reading in the front living room. She told them dinner was at seven and left her guests together.

Upstairs, Evie showered, slipped into white cotton cargo pants and an emerald-green collared T-shirt and low-heeled sandals. She raked a comb through her hair, applied a little makeup and headed from her room. She stopped outside Scott's bedroom. *Dinner's at seven in the main dining room. Please join me and my guests.* Her knuckles hovered millimeters from the door. *Just ask him.*

"Evie?"

He was behind her. Not in his room. She turned around, took a deep breath and told him about dinner. "So, will you join us?"

"Of course. Do I need to change?"

Evie couldn't help licking her gaze over his tall, muscular body. Jeans and T-shirt were such a great look on him. "No. I'll see you at seven." She turned on her heel and headed downstairs.

Evie loved to cook and adored her big, well-appointed kitchen. She wrapped her favorite apron over her clothes, finished off the lemon meringue pie she'd whipped up earlier that afternoon and popped it into the refrigerator to chill. The mustard beef and assortment of roasted vegetables were done within the hour and she set everything ready in the kitchen before making her way to the dining room. She set the big table for six. There would be no Trevor tonight. He'd pleaded to go to Cody's to study and promised to be home by nine o'clock. Once the buffet was set up with chilled wine and imported beer, Evie returned to the kitchen.

At five minutes to seven, people began entering the dining room. Evie noticed Scott first. Before she could say anything, the Manning sisters arrived and quickly cornered him. Evie had to smile. He took their monopoly of him with a grin and appeared to be genuinely interested in their conversation. Evie relaxed when the Kellers entered the room. Once all the introductions were done, she brought in the food and invited everyone to be seated.

It was a relaxed, enjoyable evening—mostly because Scott Jones was so effortlessly charismatic he held the attention of all her guests. Evie was as seduced by his humorous anecdotes and stories as the three other women at the table. He talked NASCAR with Trent Keller, antique restoration with Amelia Manning and the dwindling power of the European monarchies with her sister. And Evie, normally the one to hold court with her guests, remained mute and ate her dinner and simply listened to the sound of his voice.

Once dinner and dessert was done and her guests moved from the dining room and into the front living area, Evie began clearing up the dishes and remaining food. Busy with her task, she didn't immediately notice how Scott had stayed behind and now stood in the doorway, watching her intently. Very intently. His blue-eyed gaze scorched over her as if they were linked by a thread of fire.

"Need some help?"

No. "Ah—sure."

"So," he said quietly as he grabbed a stack of dishes. "Flora tells me you need a hand putting up some decorations?"

Evie stilled. "Trevor's going to help me."

His brows rose over those remarkable eyes. "Trevor's not here, though."

He had a point. "Well, no. I can get to it tomorrow night."

"Trevor mentioned he had a party at his friends' place tomorrow night?"

And another point. "Oh, yes, that's right." She didn't want his help and didn't want to question why. "I'll do it some other time, then."

"No time like the present," he said easily. "Flora and Amelia are keen to see them up."

He was right. She had promised to finish decorating the house. Not accepting his help made her sound foolish and neurotic. "Well, okay. I could use some help later."

That settled Evie headed back to the kitchen with her arms loaded. Scott was close behind her and then made another trip to collect what remained. He stayed and helped stack the dishwasher, and Evie was so excruciatingly aware of his every movement she had to stop herself from staring at him.

Once the kitchen was cleaned up, Evie turned toward him. "There's a ladder in the shed outside. Perhaps you could—"

"Sure," he said quickly, and disappeared through the back door.

While he was gone Evie retrieved a box of decorations from the cupboard beneath the stairs. When he returned she was waiting in the front foyer, armed with scissors, double-sided tape, a packet of small nails and a hammer.

Scott held the ladder in the crook of his arm. "So, where do you want me?"

A loaded question.

Evie cleared her throat and pointed to the archway above. "I'd like this put up there," she said, and pulled a wreath from the box.

Scott placed the ladder in the doorway. He took the wreath and held out his hand for nails and the hammer. "Just tell me where," he said, and climbed up the steps.

Evie stood still and gave instructions. *Not so easy.* When he reached the top step, her eyes were directly in line with his groin. *Not easy at all.* She looked toward the floor and examined the rubber stops at the bottom of the ladder and counted the markings on the timber floorboards. She looked anywhere but straight ahead. But temptation grabbed hold of the blood in her veins and she looked up and almost lost her breath when he raised his arms to knock in the small nails and his jeans slipped fractionally, exposing that glorious, beautiful belly, and her breath suddenly caught.

"Evie?"

She jerked her head up so fast she almost snapped her neck. As he looked down at her, Evie knew she'd been caught staring.

He smiled. "I need another nail."

She pulled another from the box and dropped it into his outstretched palm.

"That should do it," he said, and came down the steps. "Anything else?"

Evie dived for the box and withdrew another green and bronze festive wreath. "This," she said, taking a breath. "On the front door."

While he attended to the door, Evie looked inside the box. *Mistletoe.* The everlasting plastic type sat in a bunch at the bottom of the box. The last thing she wanted were sprigs of the kissing plant hung up at every doorway. She shoved it back into the corner of the box and pulled out three lengths of long green garland instead. "This goes in the front living room," she explained. "Along the picture rail."

"Lead the way."

She tucked the box under her arm and walked toward the front room. There was no sign of her guests and she assumed they'd all retired for the evening. It took about fifteen minutes to hang the remaining garlands. When they were done she adjusted a few lights on the Christmas tree and pretended not to notice his movements when he folded up the ladder and placed the hammer and tape back in the box. The tree really was spectacular—now all she needed to do was begin her shopping and put some parcels beneath it.

"What about this?" He pulled something out of the box. The mistletoe.

In his hands, the small plastic greenery seemed to be laughing in her face. She should have tossed the stuff in the garbage bin. "I don't think so."

He grinned. "You're sure?"

"Positive."

"Not even one piece?"

He was still grinning. *Probably amused by the look on my face.* Evie tried to keep her voice light. "If that goes up I'm sure the Manning sisters will be chasing you around the house for the next three weeks."

He smiled, showing off that dimple, making her head spin. He twirled the bunch of plastic sprigs between his fingers. "I guess it's fortunate I have a thing for older women."

"It's still not a good idea," she managed to say, and fought back the feeling she was treading into deep water. But she felt the awareness in the air—it pulsed between them, catching them both, fanning the flames of an attraction she somehow knew was unmistakable.

He smiled again and tossed the item back in the box. "It's your call."

Yes, it is. "Well, thank you for your help. Good night."

His brows rose fractionally. "Are you sending me off to bed, Evie?"

She colored wildly, feeling the heat, feeling the air thicken. "Of course not. I just—"

A door slammed at the back of the house. Trevor. Evie made a sound of almost palpable relief. "That's my son. I should go and see if he's eaten." She turned and walked away but stopped at the threshold. *I'm being such an idiot.*

When she turned back, he was still standing by the box. "Peppermint tea," she said loosely, shaking her shoulders. "I'm making some if you're interested."

He smiled and the lethal dimple showed itself again. "Coffee would be better."

"Sure...coffee."

Evie headed upstairs and felt him in her wake. Trevor was standing by the open refrigerator when she walked into the kitchenette. "Hungry?" she asked her son.

Trevor shook his head. "Not anymore," he replied before he shoved a piece of cold homemade pizza into his mouth.

Scott was behind her and she heard him laugh softly. Evie ignored the way her belly rocked at the sound and concentrated on her son. "I can make you some—"

"I think I'm gonna crash," Trevor said.

Stay. But she didn't say it. Didn't dare admit she needed her son's presence to shield her from her ever-growing awareness around Scott. She bid him good-night and waited until she heard his bedroom door shut before filling the jug. Scott sat in a chair, the same one he'd occupied that morning.

He looks so good in my kitchen. I could get used to him being in my kitchen.

Evie rested her hand on the stainless-steel appliance. She was appalled by her thoughts. And knew she had to say something. "Scott, I—"

"Evie, I—"

Both stopped, both looked, both had something to say. "You go," she said quickly.

He nodded and placed his elbows on the table. "Okay. Something is happening here."

She caught her breath. "It is?"

"You know it. Downstairs...and earlier today...it was there again."

Denial burned on the edge of her tongue. But instead she nodded. She wanted the truth out there. Truth always worked.

"So, what should we do about it?"

Evie's cheeks burned. "Do? Nothing. It's just…"

"Attraction," he finished for her. "Yeah…and it's powerful, Evie."

He *was* attracted to her? Evie could barely contain the emotions and feelings running riot through her entire body. She'd suspected it. She'd certainly felt it herself. But to suddenly know this gorgeous man felt it, too, made her head spin.

She drew in a breath. "We have to keep it in perspective," she said evenly. "I mean, you're only here for three weeks. And you're Callie's brother. And I'm hardly your type."

That made him smile. "You know my type?"

"I imagine someone your own age would suit."

"You're an ageist?"

"I'm a realist," she replied, feeling hot all over because she was sure he was laughing at her. "I'm… And you're… It's a crazy idea."

"Probably," he said quietly. "But sometimes crazy ideas are the most fun."

Evie skinned burned. "I'm not looking for fun."

His eyes widened. "What are you looking for?"

"Nothing," she said flatly. "I have everything I need."

"Then you're one of the lucky few."

"What does that mean?" she asked quickly.

"It means that most of us are looking for something— friendship, success, love, sex."

Evie swallowed hard. "And you're looking for sex?" she replied, and couldn't believe the words were coming out of her mouth.

"As much as the next guy, I suppose."

It was a fairly relaxed response—when Evie knew there was nothing relaxed about what was happening between them. A fire was building and they were both fanning the flames.

He wants me? My God, I've forgotten how it feels to be wanted.

For a second she thought about Gordon. About wanting him. About how good it had felt. And then her thoughts shifted again to Scott and suddenly she didn't want to think, or make comparisons or imagine for even a moment that what she'd had with her husband could ever be replaced.

"I'm not interested in…" She colored, felt the heat rise up her neck. "I'm not in a position to pursue something that's… What I'm trying to say is that I'm not interested in casual sex."

Scott linked his hands together and looked at her with such burning intensity Evie couldn't drag her gaze away. "Believe me, Evie, if I made love to you, there would be nothing casual about it."

I'm dreaming this…that's the only explanation. "But we—"

"But we won't," he said decisively. "Yeah, I get that." He stared directly into her eyes. "I'm not entirely clueless, Evie. I have figured out what kind of woman you are, even if my sister hadn't pointed out your virtues."

"Callie said something to you about me?" she asked, mortified, and not quite believing they were having this conversation. Her virtues? How dull and unexciting did that make her sound? "What did she say?"

"Word for word?" he asked, smiling. "That you were likable and generous."

Definitely dull and unexciting. "Damned with faint praise," she said, and cradled her mug.

"Not accurate, then?"

Evie laughed. "Oh, I'd say it's accurate. But it makes me sound old and boring."

Scott unlinked his hands and leaned back in his chair. "How old are you?" he asked quietly. "Thirty-five? Thirty-six?"

"Six."

"Which hardly qualifies you for a walker."

She liked how his words made her feel—liked the slight grin on his face, which teased the edges of his dimple. "I suppose not. But, you know, despite what your sister said about me, I'm not always as nice as people make out."

"Must be hard living up to the expectations of others."

Evie looked at him, tilted her head and smiled. "I guess you'd know a bit about that yourself?"

"I would?"

She shrugged and then narrowed her gaze, trying to focus her thoughts into words. "You're expected to race into burning buildings, climb up trees to rescue kittens and risk your life for people you don't know simply because of the profession you chose. Sounds like you've got the tougher gig."

"It's just a job," he said flatly.

"And you love it?" she asked.

"I couldn't imagine doing anything else."

"Because you're addicted to the risks?"

He looked at her a little warily. "Because I took an oath to preserve life and property."

"Someone else's life," she said automatically. "Someone else's property."

"You disapprove?" he shot back, sharper, as if she'd hit a button inside him.

Evie took a moment. She took a few steps forward and pulled out a chair. As she sat she considered what she was about to say. She didn't want to sound irrational—she didn't want to admit to something and give Scott a window into her fears and thoughts. She'd said too much already.

But suddenly she wanted to say it. She wanted to get it out. The words formed on the edge of her tongue, and before the sensible part of her kicked in, she spoke. "My husband was an Emergency Services volunteer. One night there was a cyclone moving off the coast and he went out to help evacuate the holiday park because the strong winds were overturning trailers and camper vans. He was killed preserving life and property. And I was left to raise our son alone."

Chapter Four

Scott heard the pain in Evie's voice, felt it through to the marrow in his bones. It rang in his ears over and over. And his career suddenly loomed like a red flag. Her husband had died serving the community and he knew without a doubt that a firefighter from California didn't have a chance of being part of her life.

Not that he wanted to get involved...he was just thinking, wondering. And as he looked at her and saw the pain in her green eyes, Scott felt compelled to tell her he was sorry for her loss, but he knew the words would be inadequate.

"You're angry?" he said, not quite sure where he was going.

She shook her head quickly, as if she knew it was what he'd ask. "It's difficult to explain. I...sometimes I feel... I feel like..."

"Like what? I'm listening," Scott assured her when her voice faded.

She met his eyes directly, and his heart knocked behind his ribs. Strange, he thought, watching her, waiting for her to speak. Everything about Evie called out to some kind of inner radar inside him. Despite her outer layer of easygoing friendliness, Scott knew, without being sure how, that she was a complex woman who felt things deeply.

She took a long breath. "I feel like I should have known something was going to happen."

There was guilt in her words. And Scott knew guilt all too well. "You couldn't possibly have foreseen the future."

"I'm not sure. Gordon and I had this connection. It was strong—unbreakable. We always knew when something wasn't right and when we needed each other."

His insides heated up. She'd obviously loved her husband deeply. The notion shouldn't mean anything to him. Strangely, it did. "But?"

She shrugged. "But that night it felt different. The cyclone had been upgraded three times in the twelve hours prior to the evacuation of the holiday park. We were taping windows and clearing the yard of potential flying objects, like garden chairs, when the call out came. He left immediately."

Scott's skin prickled. "He left you here alone?"

She shook her head. "No," she said quickly. "Noah was here. His ex-wife and eldest daughter were away at the time, so he came over to give Gordon a hand preparing for the storm. After Gordon left I went downstairs and sat by the front window, looking out into the dark, listening to the wind and rain."

"And waiting?" Scott asked, prompting her.

She nodded. "Yes. I waited for hours," she said quietly. "When he didn't come home, I knew. I knew before the police arrived. I sensed it. I felt it." Evie shook her head, as if she were shaking the words out, ridding herself of the memories. "I don't know why I'm telling you this." She sighed heavily. "I haven't talked about Gordon's accident for years."

"Maybe because you're always the listener?"

She looked surprised by his question. "How did you know that?"

"It's not hard to figure," he replied, toying with his cup, wanting to keep her talking because being around her reached a place inside him that suddenly felt a whole lot more powerful than simply physical attraction. "You run this place—it's the kind of job that makes you the one who gets to listen to the lives of everyone else. And generally people like to talk about themselves."

"That's true," she said. "Do you?"

He shrugged. "Depends on who's doing the listening."

"You've got my attention," she said quietly.

Scott looked at her. "And you've got mine."

The air between them changed again, shifting on some kind of invisible and powerful axis. He knew she felt it as much as he did.

"Which kind of brings us back to what we were talking about before," she said, smiling fractionally, though he sensed the last thing she wanted to do was smile. "I'm thinking we should just keep a lid on whatever is happening."

Sex was happening, he thought. Or at least the idea of sex. That's all it was, surely? But she didn't want it to happen. And he knew it *couldn't* happen. "Sure."

Evie took a deep breath. "Good. We both agree it's the sensible course of action."

He bit back a smile. "Very sensible."

Scott watched her, fascinated, as her skin flushed beneath his gaze. She really was remarkably sexy. There was nothing obvious about Evie Dunn. But she possessed a latent sensuality that brimmed beneath the surface and it had quickly mesmerized him.

"Do something with me tomorrow?"

She stared at him. "Do what?"

"Sailboarding," he said easily, not sure why he was suggesting it.

She shook her head. "I couldn't possibly."

"Why not? Do you already have plans?"

"I'm not exactly the adventurous type."

"It's not bungee jumping, Evie. It's a board, a sail, some wind and a bit of balance. Can you swim?" he asked.

Evie nodded. "Of course."

"Then you can probably sailboard," he said, and an idea formed in his head. "I'll teach you."

She didn't bother to conceal her surprise. "I don't think it's a good idea."

"Sure it is," he said easily, and smiled. "I'm on vacation, remember? You don't want to ruin it by refusing to help me enjoy the sights of your little town, do you?"

"No," she said after a long, cautious-looking moment. Finally she smiled back. "I guess I don't."

"If it makes you feel better, we could get Trevor to come as a chaperone?" he suggested, smiling to himself.

She frowned and he liked the way her nose wrinkled when she worked out he was teasing her. "We *hardly* need a chaperone," she said purposely, and her green eyes lit up with a kind of defiance. "Okay, I'll do it."

Scott wasn't sure what the feeling was that pitched in his chest. Relief maybe? The idea of spending time with Evie pleased him. Too much.

They said good-night, lingered over the words for a few moments before Scott left the kitchen and headed to his room. He had a restless night. The time zone difference caught up with him and he spent most of the night lying on his back in the big bed, staring at the ceiling. And he thought about Evie just a few doors away.

He'd planned to go into Bellandale the following morning and hire a car. He needed wheels—and didn't want to spend every day until the wedding hanging around the B and B like loose change.

He'd come to Crystal Point for his sister's wedding. Only he hadn't expected Evie.

Scott tossed in the bed, looked at the digital clock on the small table to his left and pumped the pillow with his fist. *I've had too much sleep...and too much coffee...and way too much Evie for one evening.*

He thumped the pillow again, dropped his head back and closed his eyes.

Why is there a motorcycle in my driveway?

And not the basic model, either. This was huge and powerful and clearly designed for cruising. Evie grabbed the pair of planet-friendly shopping bags from the passenger seat of her Honda and stared at the big, noisy-looking machine parked in front of her studio. She figured out who the culprit was once she went upstairs and spotted two helmets on the kitchen table and a leather jacket hanging on the back of a chair.

She didn't have to wait long for Scott to emerge. He stood in the doorway, one shoulder resting against the frame. He wore a pale yellow T-shirt and long navy shorts—the kind made from some filmy sort of quick-dry fabric that was designed for swimming. He had trainers on his feet and sunglasses and a hat in his hand.

"Will it take you long to get ready?" he asked lazily.

Evie dropped the bags on the bench top. "Not at all. Nice bike," she said. "Yours?"

He smiled and nodded. "Just for the next three weeks.

I made a call and we can hire a board from the surf club," he said, and looked her over. "You should get changed."

She placed the perishables in the refrigerator and excused herself. In her bedroom she sat on the edge of the bed and wondered what kind of madness had taken hold of her usual good sense.

Sailboarding with Scott... She was off her trolley. She'd spent the night tossing in her bed, wondering why she'd opened up and talked to him with such intimacy. Evie never talked about herself. She never let anyone in. Oh, she made all the right noises—that was her way—but the deeper stuff, the stuff that really mattered, she kept all that guarded close to her chest. But with Scott she'd let loose about her feelings. About Gordon. About...herself.

Evie got up and shook herself and then chose shorts and a top to cover a sensible one-piece bathing suit she'd pulled from her dresser. She changed her clothes, tied her hair back into a ponytail, slapped on some sunscreen and grabbed her sun visor.

When she returned to the kitchen he was gone. Then she heard the unmistakable roar of a Harley-Davidson. She grabbed a couple of beach towels from the hall cupboard and headed outside. Evie followed the sound of the engine, saw Scott perched against the side of the motorcycle and stopped dead in her tracks.

"No way," she said, crossing her arms.

He held out a helmet. "It's only down the road. You'll be perfectly safe."

Evie looked at Scott, then the motorcycle. "I'm still not—"

"Come on," he urged as he took the towels and placed them in the storage compartment at the rear of the bike. "I won't let anything happen to you."

The way he said the words, Evie would probably have

scaled a mountain without a rope with Scott Jones beside her. She stood still while he placed the helmet on her head. It was her first time on a motorcycle, and even though the trip was brief, Evie felt the exhilaration down to her feet. She hung on to his waist, feeling the hard muscles beneath her fingers with only a thin layer of soft cotton between her hands and his stomach. She itched to stroke her fingers back and forth to *really* feel him. But she didn't because Sensible Evie Dunn didn't do that kind of thing.

When they arrived at the surf club, Scott parked the Harley and held her hand while she swung herself off.

"It's a good day for it," he said quietly. "Let's hope the wind keeps up."

He didn't release her hand and Evie didn't move, either. She looked at their hands, felt the heat between them and knew she was crazy. "Scott, I've changed my—"

"Let's go," he said, and tugged her to follow as he began walking along the pathway that led inside.

The surf club, situated at the fringe of the tourist park, was in the middle of a much-needed overhaul. Scaffolding covered the front of the building, and most of the ground level had been gutted of fittings to make way for the renovations. But there was still a small office inside the front door. A volunteer lifeguard manned the desk and within ten minutes they had the sailboard and safety vests and were heading for the beach.

The river mouth was one of Evie's favorite places. The inlet was one of the most pristine waterways in the state, and the local residents association, along with the rest of the tightly knit community, ensured that it stayed that way with regular patrols and rubbish collection. Jays Island was two hundred meters from the beach and had once been a part of the mainland. Through erosion and sand trenching to allow sugarcane ferries to pass, the island was now home to nesting herons and returning sea turtles.

"This is a great spot," he said as he placed the sailboard on the sand and flipped off his shoes. Evie did the same and her eyes almost popped out of their sockets when he pulled his T-shirt over his head and dropped it at his feet.

He had a magnificent chest and was so well cut she couldn't pull her gaze away. His smooth, bronzed skin stretched over hard, defined muscles. Flawless pecs, biceps, abs…he had it all. And she kept looking, absorbed by the beauty of him and the sheer magnitude of such physical perfection. Her fingertips tingled, as if they knew, somehow, that she wanted to reach out and touch him, to explore the contours of his smooth chest and then trace lower, down his superbly flat abdomen and lower still, to where his…

"Evie?"

His voice felt like a bucket of cold water. She knew her cheeks scorched. He smiled and she wanted the ground to open up and suck her in. "I'm…ready," she said unsteadily.

"You'll be more comfortable out of those clothes," he said, and grabbed a safety vest. "And you'll need to put this on," he said, and placed the vest beside her feet.

Evie shook her head. "I don't think—"

"Trust me," he said, so easily, so quietly, Evie's resistance faded. She grabbed the hem of her shirt and slowly pulled it over her shoulders. Scott began maneuvering the sail and didn't watch her very unseductive striptease. Evie felt a mixture of relief and mortification. She'd watched *him* as if she'd been starved of the sight of a man's body, but he showed absolutely no interest in watching *her* remove her T-shirt. Her self-esteem spiked, dwindled and then crashed to her feet as her fingers hovered on the waistband of her shorts.

Flaws. She wasn't twenty-five anymore. She had thighs she worked hard to keep toned but hadn't quite managed to maintain, and a behind she knew was fuller than what was considered fashionable. She had the body of a thirty-six-year-old woman—a woman who'd borne a child, a woman who looked and felt every year of her age as she considered the gorgeous young man beside her.

"Ready?" he asked, still not looking at her.

Why did I ever agree to this? Sand, crystal-clear water, swimsuits…she was asking for trouble. "Yes, sure." She tossed her flip-flops aside, stripped off her shorts as mechanically as she could and quickly pushed her arms into the safety vest.

"And you said you could swim?"

Her hands stilled on the task of clipping the vest and she nodded. "Reasonably."

"Good," he replied, still not looking at her. "Let's go."

Humiliation morphed into a slowly rising indignation. Okay, so her body wouldn't win prizes on the catwalk—but it wasn't totally unsightly, either.

Look at me. The words burned on the edge of her tongue. *Look at me, or I'll...*

He turned, stopped his task and straightened. And he *did* look at her. The same kind of look he'd given her in the living room the day before—long, leisurely and with the purpose of admiring. For a crazy second Evie forgot her flaws. Her perfectly respectable one-piece swimsuit suddenly felt like the most seductive piece of fabric on the planet.

Something whirled between them. Her skin prickled with awareness, her breasts felt heavy and sensitive and they pushed against the safety vest. It was as if her body had suddenly taken on a life of its own, betraying her, laughing at her.

"Come on," he said quietly, tipping his attention back to the board and forcing Evie to pull her thoughts away from having a deep lip-lock with the gorgeous man in front of her. "We don't want to waste this wind."

Evie followed him to the water's edge. And he was right—it was a good day for it. The wind was up, but the water was enticingly warm. There were a few people on the beach, some swimming, a young couple playing fetch with their dog and a stick and a trio of teenagers burying each other in the sand.

Scott explained the board and sail and how to position her feet, and Evie was agonizingly aware of his close proximity. But he was a good teacher. He was patient and considerate and didn't push her to do anything she didn't want to do. Her first attempts were disastrous, dumping them both in the water every time. But after a while she managed to maintain some balance and work the sail. She felt him behind her, felt his arms touch hers every time she maneuvered the sail to catch the breeze, and felt his chest against her back as he supported them on the narrow board.

He's really something else, she thought vaguely. The little voice in her head—the one which had been taunting her for the past two days, continued its assault. She wobbled and lost balance. Scott quickly tightened his hold and straightened the sail.

"Concentrate," he said against her ear, and Evie felt the warmth of his breath against her skin. She shivered right down her toes, despite the hot sun beating down on them. "And relax."

"I'm trying," she said, way too breathlessly, and knew she would never relax while he held her.

His body was suddenly closer, his hold firmer, more intimate, and Evie leaned into the support of his broad chest. Scott's arms cradled her like a safety net, and his hands half covered hers on the boom as the board skimmed across the water. She could feel his thighs against her bottom, and a sharp pleasure arrowed deep down in her belly. Her long-ignored libido did a wild leap, heating her blood.

And then, as he held her, it somehow became more than lust, more than an unexpected physical awakening. *Something else was happening.* Her heart pumped wildly and she experienced a kind of silly giddiness.

She leaned back farther, felt his chin against her hair and the tension suddenly coiling through his body. *Now who needs to relax?* She almost said the words. But the wind blew up and Evie pushed her concentration back to her task.

Half an hour later he steered the board toward the shore and they stepped off.

"Incredible," Evie said, and took a few much-needed breaths as Scott pulled the sailboard onto the sand. "I can't believe how much fun that was."

"Now who sounds like an adrenaline junkie?" he said, and grabbed a towel.

Evie smiled and rubbed her skin dry. "Who would have imagined it?"

He looked at her. "I think a person could spend a lifetime getting to know you, Evie, and still be surprised."

Her belly rolled. *Oh...I'm in so much trouble here.*

She did her best to ignore the ever-growing awareness and minutes later they had their clothes back on and were headed for the surf club to return the gear. When they got back to the clubhouse, there was a police car parked outside.

"Trouble?" Scott asked.

Evie shrugged, and then changed to a shake of her head when she spotted Cameron Jakowski, dressed in his regulation blue police uniform, walking across the threshold of the automatic doors.

"Hey, Evie," he greeted, juggling a few tins of paint, some brushes and a roller.

He was charming, handsome, Noah's best friend and she'd known him all her life. "What are you doing here?" she asked, stopping in front of the building.

Cameron motioned to the equipment in his hands. "We've had some graffiti problems at the community hall," he explained. "A few of the kids from the Big Brother program are giving me a hand with a quick-cover paint job." He smiled. "I ran out of paint and paintbrushes."

"Did you catch the culprits?" she asked.

"Not yet," he said, and looked at her companion inquiringly.

Evie didn't miss the look. With the sailboard between them, towels flung over their shoulders and sand-encrusted feet, she was certain Cameron's curiosity was in overdrive. She quickly made introductions and they talked for a short while about the upcoming wedding until Cameron said he had to get back to the trio of teenage boys he mentored.

"You know," he said to Scott as he opened the car door, "if you've got some free time while you're here I'm sure the boys would like to hear something about your job. We meet every Wednesday night at the community hall around seven. Guests speakers are always welcome." He dumped the equipment into the passenger seat of his police vehicle. "Evie will show you where." He looked at Evie and winked. "Let me know."

Once he'd left and they'd returned their gear, she followed Scott back to the motorcycle and waited while he tucked the towels beneath the seat. He hesitated passing her the helmet.

He looked at her oddly. "Old boyfriend?"

Evie frowned. "Cameron? God, no," she replied. "He goes through women like they're…well, let's just say he has a short attention span and leave it at that."

"And you'd like someone with a long attention span?" he asked. "Is that it?"

Evie's skin warmed and she tugged the helmet from his hands. "As much as the next woman," she said. "I'd like to think I could at least *hold* his attention for longer than one night."

Scott's heart thundered in his chest. Because Evie Dunn *had* his attention. Every last bit of it. He got on the bike and didn't move a muscle when she slid behind him and rested her hands on his waist. But he felt the heat of her touch as if she were branding him with her fingertips.

Scott sucked in a breath and started the Harley. The sooner he took her home, the better. And there would be no more sailboarding. No more skin-to-skin contact. No more having to try to keep his hands to himself. And definitely no more of that damned sexy swimsuit that revealed just enough of her to turn him inside out.

When they got back to the house, Scott heard her faintly thank him for the lesson. She took off quickly and he was glad for it. He remained outside for a while, thinking. Thinking that a hotel would be a good idea. At least it would take him away from the temptation that was Evie Dunn.

He walked around the garden, determined to get his body in check. He couldn't remember the last time he'd felt like this…maybe never. It sure as hell had snuck up on him from out of nowhere. He was lusting after something…*someone*…he couldn't have. And it was damned inconvenient.

Scott walked around the garden some more, inspecting things with more than his usual detail. Okay, so gardens weren't his thing. Evie obviously liked it, though—he could tell that by the extraordinary array of greenery and foliage and flowering plants that curved around pathways and climbed over small rock walls. There was a small wishing well in the center of the garden. An old timber plaque leaned against the edge, inviting those inclined to drop in a coin and make a wish.

"It all goes to charity."

Scott swiveled on his heel. Evie had come up behind him with the stealth of a cat. She'd changed her clothes, too. The skirt was long but somehow sexy the way it moved across her legs as she stepped closer. And her hair was loose and hung like a crown around her head, highlighting the amazing color of her eyes and perfectly shaped mouth. He couldn't drag his gaze away from her, couldn't seem to make himself look elsewhere.

"Sorry?" he heard himself say, and wondered why she'd followed him into the garden.

She pointed to the well. "The money from the wishes," she explained. "I scoop it out once a year and donate it to a charity."

"It's not making you rich, then?"

She smiled. "Hardly. People don't seem to believe in wishes all that much anymore."

Scott crossed his arms. "Do you?" he asked, feeling hot and tense all of a sudden, and knowing it was because he couldn't stop thinking about Evie's incredibly kissable mouth.

"Do I believe in wishes?" She took another step toward the well and peered into it. "I'm not sure. I guess that would be like saying I believe in magic." She stepped back. "I haven't thought about magic for a long time."

"And did you have magic with your husband?" Scott had no idea where the question came from, or why he was asking it. It was intensely personal—and way out of line. And he was even more astounded when she responded.

"A kind of magic, I suppose." She pushed a stray pebble back between the cracks in the stone pavers with her sandal. "Loving someone can feel like that—like you can do anything, achieve anything." She stopped, looked at him and gave a wry smile. "I'm not normally so sentimental."

Neither was he. But being around Evie pushed his buttons—all kinds of buttons. And some of them seemed to border on sentimental. Romantic, even. He looked at her, felt the vibrations coming off her pierce through him. Whatever he was feeling, he was pretty sure she was feeling it, too.

Somehow, she was suddenly in front of him. She looked as though she wanted to say something but stopped. Then her gaze lifted up to meet his. It was all he needed. His arms moved around her and after a flash of resistance, her palms rested against his chest.

And because he knew that at that moment there was nothing else for either of them, Scott took a breath and then kissed her amazing mouth.

Chapter Five

At some point a voice of reason was going to interrupt and tell Evie to stop kissing Scott Jones. Or get him to stop kissing her. Either way, she knew it had to end. Kisses like this weren't real. They were the stuff of fairy tales and silly movies. The kind of kisses her friend Fiona swooned over and insisted were so worth waiting for.

Okay—so being kissed by Scott *was* worth waiting for. In fact, as his mouth slanted over her own to deepen the contact, the thrill of it jolted every inch of skin covering her bones. The man certainly knew how to kiss.

But it really has to stop...

Only...when his hands moved across her hips and drew her against him, Evie lost all coherent thought. She felt his breath, his lips, his tongue, and she returned the kiss, wary at first, giving a little, taking more and really *feeling* for the first time since...forever. *No woman could resist this,* a faraway voice taunted. *No flesh-and-blood woman would want to.*

And Evie was quickly discovering she was very much a flesh-and-blood woman—and that she liked kissing Scott. She liked it so much her skin was searing and her blood felt molten hot in her veins. *Desire*...the little voice sang out again. That's what this was. *Lust. Hunger. Sex.*

Sex without love? Could she do that? Making love when love had nothing to do with it? Evie knew she simply wasn't built that way. No matter how divine his mouth felt.

He must have sensed her growing reticence because he ended the kiss and gently released her. "I'm guessing you don't think this is a good idea?"

Evie's skin heated. "Do you?"

"It's just a kiss." He said the words casually.

Evie frowned. "I'm not indiscriminate," she said as she turned her head to look back at the house, wondering if the Manning sisters were peeking through the curtains. The last thing she wanted was to get caught making out with Scott. "Anyway," she said, catching her breath and trying valiantly to look in control. "The reason I came out here was to tell you that Callie called. She's expecting you tonight about six."

He nodded. "She asked me over for dinner. Would you like to come with me?"

Sensible Evie came quickly to her rescue. Thank goodness. Otherwise she might have been tempted to say yes. "I'm teaching a class tonight."

"Too bad for me, then."

Her heart skipped, then flipped, then almost got caught in her throat. "Okay—so I'll see you later." She turned and left, not quite running, but close enough to it to look like a first-rate idiot.

Evie buried herself in her studio for the following couple of hours and waited until she heard the loud rumble of the motorcycle leaving before she returned to the house. The Kellers were out for the evening and she made swift work of preparing a light supper of soup and buttered herb bread for Flora and Amelia before heading back to the studio by seven o'clock for her class.

In her studio Evie usually found a kind of peace. Only she was so distracted the peace she craved didn't come. All she had was a head full of thoughts about Scott. She'd forgotten how good kissing was and how much she'd missed it. And she'd forgotten how it felt to be held. She'd forgotten strong arms and broad shoulders. She'd forgotten everything. No, not forgotten, but shut out...left to linger along with memories of a husband she'd loved and never imagined she could replace.

Kissing Scott had felt good. Too good. But it wouldn't go anywhere. It couldn't.

He's twenty-seven. I'm thirty-six. A math genius she wasn't—but no amount of thinking could make her see their ages as anything other than an impossible divide between two people with completely different lives. *He's all wrong for me.* A firefighter. A man with a dangerous occupation had no place in her structured, orderly world.

Evie put herself to work and began cleaning paintbrushes to fill time before her class began. She had five regular students, including her youngest sister, Mary-Jayne, and their good friend Fiona Walsh. Once her students began to arrive, she managed to clear her head and concentrate on teaching the women how to texture paint on the canvas.

"So, what's with you?" Mary-Jayne asked when the class had concluded and the last of the students had left. She always lingered for coffee and a chat.

Evie shrugged and kept pushing stools in front of empty easels. "Not a thing."

"Really? You looked about as into the class tonight as I look when I go for a dental checkup."

Evie looked at her sister. Bubbly, effervescent and lovingly indulged all her life, Mary-Jayne, or M.J. as she was affectionately called by anyone who knew her, had a history of asking completely inappropriate questions and hounding for an answer with the tenacity of a terrier.

"I'm fine."

M.J.'s incredible brows rose. "Are the hormones acting up?"

A breath stuck in Evie's throat. "What does that mean?"

"Oh, just that I heard a rumor you were shacking up with a drop-dead-gorgeous fireman."

Mortified, Evie swiveled on her heel to face her sister. "I'm not shacking up at all," she said in her best big-sister voice. "You know exactly why he…" She stopped, paused, looked at her sister and faked a smile. "It's a favor for Callie," she explained. "Her place is under renovation. Noah's got Callie's mother arriving next week and our parents' house will be packed with relatives right up until Christmas and the wedding."

"So he *is* gorgeous?"

Evie ignored the thump of her heart. "Drop by tomorrow and see for yourself."

M.J. gave a chuffed laugh. "Ha—you're not fooling me with the casual act. If your face glowed any brighter you could be used as a beacon."

Evie held her ground. "Haven't you got somewhere to be?"

M.J. laughed louder and brighter. "Of course," she replied. "Actually, I do need to get going. I've had a big order through my website and need to start on the pieces," she said, referring to her jewelry design business.

After her sister left, Evie spent some time in front of an easel. Dabbling with watercolors, she relaxed a bit and tried to lose herself in the creative process for a while. But her tension returned the moment she heard the familiar rumble of Scott's motorcycle coming up the driveway. The engine cut out quickly and before she had the opportunity to move, Evie heard a rap on the door. With only a mesh screen between them, Evie knew hiding was out of the question. She took a deep breath, and invited him inside.

"Am I interrupting?" he asked when he saw she was midbrushstroke.

Evie dropped the brush and shifted off the edge of the seat. "Not at all," she said. "I'm just playing with color— nothing serious." She stood and wiped her hands down her paint-dotted jeans. "How was your evening?"

Scott placed his helmet and keys on the bench near the door and took a few strides into the room. "Good." He smiled. "Except for Callie's cooking."

Evie smiled back. Her friend and soon-to-be sister-in-law's reputation in the kitchen was well noted. "Well, thankfully Noah can flip steaks and burgers on the barbecue if the need arises."

Scott shrugged lightly. "Your brother doesn't seem to mind that she can't cook."

"No. In fact, I think he finds it endearing," she replied.

"Well, there's certainly no doubt he loves her."

Evie nodded. "Yes, no doubt. They're very happy together. And my brother is a good man," she said directly. "He'll treat her right."

Scott's gaze narrowed fractionally. "I wasn't suggesting otherwise."

Evie lifted her shoulders and then dropped them

quickly. "Sorry—habit. Sometimes I'm overprotective of my family."

"You shouldn't apologize for that." He grabbed a stool in one deft move and placed it against the wall. "Actually," he said as he sat, "*I* find it endearing."

Evie didn't miss the hint of intimacy in his words. In fact, she knew he was being deliberately provoking. While she was trying her best to *not* think about him in that way, he didn't appear to feel the same need.

Youth and bravado.

Or just plain old male egotism running riot.

Either way, Evie knew it had to stop. Because if it didn't, she knew any moment she was going to start thinking about that scorching, toe-curling kiss again. Which simply would not do.

"I hope the bike didn't wake your guests."

She snatched a look at him, not wanting to notice the way his jeans stretched across his thighs, but noticing anyway because he was impossible to ignore. "I doubt it," she said quietly. "Trevor's staying over at Cody's, and the Manning sisters can sleep through anything." She checked her watch. "And the Kellers have gone into town for dinner and a movie."

"So we're all alone?"

More intimacy. More curled toes. More everything. Evie fought to catch her breath before it left her throat. "Like I said, Amelia and Flora are inside asleep."

"And they can sleep through anything?"

Her heart skipped. "What did you have in mind?" she asked, although she couldn't believe the words came out.

"Come for a ride with me?"

She straightened, narrowed her gaze and automatically looked at her watch. "It's ten o'clock."

"Do you have a curfew?" he asked.

Evie shook her head. "Of course not. It's just that I couldn't—"

"I promise the bike won't turn into a pumpkin after midnight," he said, smiling just enough for her to see his dimple. "And I won't turn into a frog."

"You're mixing your fairy tales," Evie said. "*Cinderella* and *The Frog Prince*—both favorites of mine—but both very different stories."

"The ending's the same, though, isn't it?"

Evie drew in a breath. "Yes."

"So come with me?" He looked at her with searing intensity. "I feel like a walk on the beach."

Evie squashed back the feeling of anticipation weaving up her back. But she willed herself not to be tempted. "Not a good idea."

He chuckled and it was such a sexy sound Evie could barely stand still in her own skin. "Evie, there's something unique about you that makes me want to get to know you better."

Evie held her breath. The man was seductive and mesmerizing. And she was in serious trouble of falling head over heels in lust. "We agreed that we wouldn't get involved."

"It's just an invitation to walk along the beach," he said easily. "Not a marriage proposal."

She twisted her fingers together, determined to do something with her ridiculously unsteady hands. *I am behaving like a first-rate fool.* But her resistance lingered. Evie knew what would happen if they were alone together on a deserted beach late at night. They might kiss again, and touch… Scott might take her in his arms and she would go willingly to wherever he led her. Perhaps they would make love on the sand.

He studied her face, absorbing every feature and making her hot all over. "Okay," he said so quietly Evie took a small step toward him. If he was going to speak she wanted to hear what he had to say. When he pushed himself off the stool, they were only a few feet apart. "Evie…"

She looked up, met his gaze and swayed forward.

"You're very talented."

Not what she was expecting. And he now looked above her head and at the many paintings hung around the room, and she hadn't expected that, either. "Thank you."

He stepped to the side and walked between the free-standing easels. "Do you sell much of your work?"

"Not really."

"Why not?" he asked, and stood in front of a trio of watercolor landscapes on one wall. "These are excellent."

Evie followed his steps. "Do you have an interest in art?"

He shrugged. "I know what I like. Although I'm no expert. You have an amazing gift."

A gift? It had been such a long time since anyone had called it that. Gordon had, a lifetime ago. He'd been her greatest supporter and in many ways her muse. He'd pushed her to work harder, to give her best every time she put brush to canvas. But his death had killed off something inside her, too. Evie hadn't stopped painting completely, although the need to showcase her work had been left behind with all the rest of her ambition. Nowadays she only painted for herself, and with the B and B, her son and the classes she taught occupying most of her time, painting for herself had become little more than an occasional whim.

"I don't get to paint as much as I used to."

He half turned and faced her. "Why not?"

Evie shrugged. "No time."

"Although you used to have time," he said quietly, and motioned to the nearly two dozen frames hanging around the room and the stack of unfinished pieces lying against the wall in a dark corner. "Judging by the look of things."

She shrugged again, feeling the bite of criticism. "Do you mean before I became a single mother and had to run this place by myself?"

He turned back to her immediately and both brows shot up. "Is that your way of telling me to mind my own business?"

Evie glared at him. "Would it make much difference?"

"I can be as sensitive as the next guy," he said easily, looking her over in that way which made her skin burn. "Try me."

She went to reply, and then stalled. Evie rarely talked about her work. Actually, she *never* talked about her work. But there was an edge of something she couldn't quite recognize skirting the mood between them, and she felt reluctant to break the link. Evie clutched her arms around her waist and wandered toward an unfinished piece on a large easel.

"I don't paint like I used to. I don't seem to have the heart for it anymore." She let out a heavy breath. "I don't think I've admitted that to anyone before."

He came beside her and looked at the picture. "You lost your drive?"

"I guess. When I was young I lived to paint. I couldn't wait to create the next piece, to see where the brush would take me. I'd spend hours in here, mixing colors, sketching and thinking up new ways to be bold and innovative. And then I stopped. After Gordon…well, I just couldn't seem to…" She paused and looked at the unfinished pieces in the corner. "I just couldn't finish anything."

"Do you still enjoy painting?"

She glanced sideways. "In here I do." She tapped her temple softly. "But in here…" Her hand came to her chest.

"I don't have the feeling in here. And that's where it really comes from. Creativity is all about heart."

"And your heart is still broken?"

Evie swayed sideways. The need to be held by his strong arms suddenly overwhelmed her. She'd never ask it. Never show it. But it pierced through her with razor-sharp precision. "My heart is full," she said quietly. "With my son, my family, this place I've been blessed to live in. Plus, I have my students, and teaching gives me great satisfaction."

He looked at her, meeting her gaze head-on. "There's a 'but' in there, Evie. And there's no shame in that. If you love to paint, then that's exactly what you should do. You owe it to yourself to try and find your heart again."

She felt the sting in his words, although she was certain he hadn't meant it that way. She knew she was being overly sensitive, but she bit back anyway. "I wouldn't expect someone like you to understand."

"Why not?" he shot back quickly. "Because you think I'm just a grunt who runs into burning buildings for a living?"

He was stung by her comment, and part of her couldn't blame him. Her words *had* sounded condescending and she wondered why she'd said them. Normally she was rational and sensible. But she was mad at him for making her explain her thoughts and feelings about her painting. It wasn't open for discussion. Not ever.

"I don't want to talk about it," she said, and pushed herself to move away from him. She grabbed a bundle of paintbrushes, took them to the sink and dropped them into a plastic container. "I don't talk about *me*," she admitted, still by the sink and without the courage to turn around and face him. "Not to anyone."

"Then I guess we're a lot alike."

She snapped her neck around and managed a tiny smile.

Were they alike? Was that why she sensed an invisible thread of connection between them? And why it felt like way more than physical attraction? She felt something, a kind of link with Scott, but it was hazy, like drifting through fog while listening to the sound of someone's voice.

"Do you ever envy those people who can express every emotion and feeling they have whenever they're having it?" she asked. "Sometimes I do. My sister M.J. says whatever she wants regardless of the consequences—and she gets away with it. While my other sister, Grace, is about as uptight and closed off as you can get."

"And you?"

She shrugged, turned around and rested against the bench top. "I'm somewhere in the middle. Reliable and predictable, following rules, making sure everyone else is taken care of."

"There's nothing wrong with following rules, Evie. Or being reliable," he said, and crossed his arms. "You don't have to be reckless to lead a fulfilling life."

Evie stared at him. It seemed a strange thing for him to say. He was a firefighter. He lived his life on the very edge of danger. What would he know about following the rules? Unless she'd completely misjudged him.

"You sound as if you're talking from experience."

He lifted his shoulders and dropped them with a heavy breath. "I just know that sometimes being reckless hurts people. Risking everything can be disastrous. Often someone else is left to pick up the pieces, and that's not a great legacy for anyone to leave behind."

He was right. And it was exactly why she always lived her life in a sensible, orderly fashion. Sure, there were no risks, but there was also no chance of hurting the people she loved. Strange, but she'd imagined Scott as a risk taker.

"I didn't think you'd be so…so…"

"So what?" he asked.

"So sensible," she replied. "Your job, your age, I thought you'd be—"

"I'm twenty-seven," he said, cutting her off. "Not seventeen. In fact, I'll be twenty-eight in a couple of months. As for my job, sure, it can be dangerous—but so can working on a high-rise or driving a truck. I haven't any illusions and I don't take the potential dangers of my job lightly. And I certainly wouldn't expect anyone…" He stopped, looked at her and twisted his mouth for a moment. "I wouldn't expect anyone…*any woman* to wait around for that late-night call saying I'd been injured, or worse."

Her chest tightened. She knew that call. She'd experienced it firsthand. "Is that why your last relationship didn't work out?"

"We worked together, lived together—I couldn't treat her like the rest of the crew. I wanted to keep her safe. She put up with twelve months of what she called my outdated macho crap and left."

Evie had always secretly liked that outdated macho crap. "And you won't get seriously involved with anyone while you're a firefighter?"

He shrugged. "No."

Part of her was acutely disappointed—the other was impressed by his integrity and she admired his principles. A niggling thought suddenly attached itself to the back corner of her mind. *If only Gordon had thought like that. I wouldn't be a widow—my son would still have his father.*

"You might fall in love?"

His blue eyes seared into hers. "I might."

"And if you do?"

He shrugged again. "No point worrying about something that hasn't happened."

Evie read between the lines. So there was no middle road. He was a man with strong convictions, and her admiration spiked. She was like that, too. She'd made a commitment to raise her son and be the best mother she could be after Gordon had died. All her energy, all her love had gone into her parenting. The good daughter, the good mother, the good widow.

And now Scott had walked into her life and she felt like abandoning every single of one of her principles and allowing herself to get swept up in his arms. Evie had never experienced anything quite like it before. Certainly she'd had desire for Gordon and enjoyed making love with him. But this feeling…this low-down-in-her-belly kind of slowly building craving was suddenly all she could think about. All she could want.

"I have to go," she said. So quietly she wasn't sure he heard her.

But he had. He grasped her arm as she made a move to leave. "Don't run away."

Evie's breath caught in her throat. "I have to," she whispered.

"You act like I'm some sort of threat to you," he said, and rubbed the underside of her arm with his fingers. "I'm not. At least, not intentionally."

"That's not it. I'm a threat to myself," she admitted, hypnotized by his gentle caress. "I'm feeling so… I'm not sure what exactly. But I know I shouldn't be feeling whatever it is. Maybe that doesn't make sense—I don't know. I only know that you'll be gone in three weeks and I'll still be here. And I have to make sure I'll be here with myself and with my life intact."

His touch continued to hold her captive. "I have no intention of taking advantage of you, Evie," he said softly, his voice as seductive as the soft stroke of his fingertips.

"And if you feel like you've been suddenly hit by a freight train—well, frankly, so do I."

She looked up. He wanted to kiss her...and Evie wanted it, too. She willed herself not to feel such a longing, to look at him and not see a man she desired more than she'd imagined possible. But her body was in control. Her body was calling all the shots.

Her breasts felt heavy, as if they knew she wanted him. Still, he only touched her arm, gently rubbing the soft skin. But it was enough. Her nipples peaked, tightening so much she knew they were clearly visible through the thin cotton of her T-shirt and lace-cup bra. Her belly dipped and rolled on a wave of desire so strong she wondered if her legs might give way.

"I can't...I want to...but I can't," she whispered. "I'm an ordinary woman and I lead an ordinary life... Don't ask me to be something other than who and what I am."

Scott's fingers stilled. "I wouldn't. I won't. I get you, Evie," he said as he released her. "I get the way you live your life—I get that you had to do whatever it took to work your way through losing your husband. I understand why you always do the right thing, the sensible thing. And because you're right—I am only here for three weeks and the two of us getting involved would not be sensible. It might be incredible...it might be mind-blowing. But it wouldn't be *sensible*."

He stepped back and put space between them. Then he stepped away and grabbed his helmet and keys. When he reached the door he stopped and half turned. "And, Evie— there's *nothing* ordinary about you," Scott said quietly.

Once he'd gone through the door, Evie's shaky legs found a chair and she slumped back with a heavy breath. Scott Jones was one heck of a nice guy. *And I'm falling for him hook, line and sinker.*

Chapter Six

On Saturday morning Evie headed into town and shopped at her favorite organic grocery store. When she got home Scott's motorcycle was notably absent and she experienced a mix of emotions. He'd gone for an early run that morning and they'd barely crossed paths over breakfast. She attended to her guests during lunch and, after catching up on a few domestic chores, spent the afternoon in her studio.

By the time she'd showered and changed her clothes, it was nearly five o'clock. She heard Scott's motorcycle return and then the sound of feet on the stairwell followed by a couple of doors opening and closing and the distinct hiss of the shower in the guest bathroom.

She walked into the kitchenette and saw her son. "Are you getting ready soon?"

He half frowned from his spot near the sink. "I wish I could stay home."

"No chance. Your grandparents are expecting you."

Trevor's lanky shoulders popped up and down. "It was just a thought."

"And I *thought* you liked your grandparents?" she suggested quietly, smiling.

He grinned. "You know I do. But there are basketball tryouts coming up before the school terms out and I figured I should practice if I want to make the team for next year."

A team? And sports? She planted her hands on her hips. "Okay…where's my son and what have you done with him?"

Trevor laughed. "It's still me. I just thought I might try out, that's all… You know, get outdoors for a while."

Her smart, computer geek son certainly surprised her. "I think…I think it's a great plan."

He shrugged, looking embarrassed all of a sudden. "Yeah, well, it was just an idea. I probably won't make the cut. You know I suck at sports. But Scott said he'd help."

Scott…

Of course. Her fatherless son would think Scott Jones hung the moon.

She ached inside thinking about it. "You're a shoe-in, I'm sure. Now go and get dressed. You've got fifteen minutes."

He dragged his feet as he left, and Scott came into the room a couple of minutes later. Evie pretended to busy herself by mopping up a nonexistent spill on the draining board. The air between them was thick. Stupid, she thought, to have tension when there were no words said and barely any eye contact. Evie slanted a look in his direction while she folded a tea towel. He looked so good in dark olive chinos and pressed white shirt. Too good. Everything about him oozed sex—the way he moved, the way he spoke, the way his hair flicked across his forehead.

"What time are we expected?" he asked.

She collected her thoughts. "Around six," she replied. They were going to her parents' house for a barbecue and Evie liked that he'd dressed up a bit. He looked older somehow. And then she felt absurd for daring to admit such a thing mattered to her. *I shouldn't be thinking that.* They weren't dating, they weren't anything really. Barely acquaintances who would soon be related only because of a marriage between their siblings. *One incredible kiss doesn't make a relationship.*

"Trevor was telling me how you're helping him to get on the basketball team."

He glanced at her and shrugged. "Just giving him a few tips."

"You were a jock in high school, right?" she asked directly. "And good at everything?"

Scott looked at her oddly. She wished she knew him better. Wished she could figure out what he was thinking behind those glittering blue eyes.

When he didn't respond she continued. "It's just that Trevor isn't usually a…sporty sort of teenager. He's more at home with his video games or computer. But I understand why he'd want to spend time with you."

He didn't move. "You do?"

"Sure. I mean…he doesn't get a lot of adult male company. Other than Noah and my dad. And you're so…so…"

"So?"

She ignored his question. Ignored the way her heart pounded like a jackhammer. And she stuck to her point. "I don't expect you to entertain my son while you're here, that's all."

He swayed fractionally on his heels, and a semismile tucked at the corner of his mouth. "He's a good kid."

"I know that."

"So I don't mind helping him out."

What if I don't want my son getting attached to you?

Thankfully Trevor loped through the doorway and announced he was ready to go. Her son wore the clothes she'd put out on his bed and had managed to tame his unruly hair with what looked like a bucket of hair gel. Evie grabbed her tote, ran her hands down the front of her pale green dress and grabbed the car keys from the table.

Once they were outside she held out the keys toward Scott. "Why don't you drive? I'll sit in the back," she explained. "You've both got longer legs than me." She pointed to her son's lanky pins but refused to ogle Scott. "So let's go. I'll give directions."

The drive to her parents' sprawling double-story home took only minutes. Scott was out before her and quickly opened the back door. He took her hand to steady her as she got out, and Evie felt the electricity coursing between them as their fingers connected. She caught her breath as a rush of blood raced across her skin. He saw it though, and even if he hadn't Evie was certain he could have felt the heat from it. And he didn't release her, at least not straightaway. And Evie didn't pull away, either. She remembered the vow she'd made to keep him at a distance, to not get involved, and all her resolutions disappeared. He was simply holding her hand, and all Evie could think about was how much she didn't want him to let her go. Not ever.

Trevor said something and Scott dropped his hand and closed the passenger door while Evie made a quick escape around to the other side of the car. She made it into the house in record time and didn't wait for either Scott or her son, figuring they could find their own way to the back patio. For now, Evie simply wanted to get away.

Her mother, Barbara, was in the kitchen and she headed straight for her and hung on to a hug a little longer than normal. She apologized for not helping with the cooking, and her mother quickly brushed off her concerns and told her that Grace, who'd arrived from New York a few days earlier, had helped her prepare the food for the thirty or so guests expected to arrive within the next half hour. Evie immediately began decorating a cheesecake.

"Have you spoken to your sister recently?" her mother asked, passing Evie an apron.

"Not since the day she arrived home. Why?"

Barbara shrugged. "She doesn't seem herself."

She's not the only one. "I'll talk to her," she assured her mother, and got the chance about five minutes later when her sister entered the room.

It was hard not to notice when Grace Preston entered a room—because she was simply stunning. Beautiful in a classic, old movie star kind of way. Beside her, Evie spent most of her time feeling about as plain as an old shoe. In designer jeans, three-inch heels Evie knew would have cost the earth and a red blouse that looked as though it wouldn't dare crease because Grace simply wouldn't allow it, her sister was a picture of elegance. No one pulled off wearing jeans like Grace. Four years younger than Evie, she worked for a large brokerage house in New York and had arrived in Crystal Point a few days earlier. She was successful, well educated and to those who didn't know her, about as warm as an Arctic winter. But Evie knew her and loved her and had always been able to get past her sister's cool reserve.

"This is the first time you've been home for Christmas in a while," Evie said once their mother had left the kitchen.

"I promised Noah I'd be here for the wedding. And the office closes down over Christmas," Grace explained.

Evie nodded. "Will you be back for Dad's party?" she

asked, thinking about their father's sixty-fifth birthday coming up in a few months.

"I'll do my best," Grace replied.

Evie began her task of piping cream onto the cheesecake. "Is anything wrong, Gracie?"

Grace looked at her. "Not at all."

"Work's okay?"

She shrugged again, but Evie wasn't fooled. "The same."

"And Erik?" she asked of her sister's lawyer boyfriend.

"Gone," Grace replied. "Months ago."

Typical that her sister hadn't mentioned it. "Bad breakup?"

"Not especially. What about you?" Grace asked, raising both her immaculate brows. "Are *you* okay?"

Evie stopped her task. "Of course. You know me," she said with a small laugh. She put down the piping bag. "Why do you ask?"

"M.J. mentioned something," Grace replied. "About Callie's b—"

"Not you, too," Evie groaned, cutting off her sister's words. "It's nothing. There's nothing going on. Nothing at all. Absolutely nothing."

"So it's *nothing?*" Grace asked with a wry smile. "Despite his obvious attributes?"

Evie colored hotly. "You met him, then?"

Grace nodded. "Noah introduced me. He seems…nice."

Evie managed a smile. Her sister didn't hand out compliments often. "My son thinks so, too."

It sounded snippy and sour put like that and she was instantly ashamed of herself.

Grace didn't let up, either. "But you don't?"

Evie made a face. "Well, of course I think he's…" She stopped and her voice trailed off. She quickly took a breath and tried again. "Okay, he's...*fine,* obviously," she admitted. "And that's all I'm going to say about it."

"Who's fine?"

They both turned their heads at the sound of Callie's voice. Her husky lilt echoed across the tiled floor, and Evie wished that same floor would open up and swallow her whole. "Um—no one. So, how's the party going out there?"

Callie made a face as she moved into the kitchen. "A few of the men have gone to the games room for a game of pool," she said, and rolled her eyes. "And you know how competitive Noah and Cameron are—they turn it into a blood sport. Although I told Scott to go easy on them because they're poor losers."

Evie's interest spiked. "He plays well?"

"My brother is one of those infuriating people who are good at everything."

Evie's insides crunched. Hadn't she said that to Scott only an hour earlier when they'd been discussing Trevor? She stole a look at Grace, and her sister raised a questioning brow before Evie turned back to decorating the cheesecake. Grace left the room a few moments later, pleading the need to observe their brother and Cameron get beaten at pool, and Evie watched Callie attempt to fill a piping bag with cream. She took pity on her and took over the task.

"Thanks," Callie said quietly and stepped back, resting her hips against the countertop. "Evie, can I ask you something?"

"Sure," she replied. "Shoot."

"Are you okay with having my brother at your house?"

Evie stilled, felt her breath get lost in her throat and tried desperately not to show it. "Of course. Why?"

"He said something about maybe moving into a hotel while he's here."

Evie's knees risked failure and she pushed herself

against the bench to stay upright. "Oh, really?" She tried to make her voice as light as possible, tried to make out as if Callie's announcement hadn't shaken her up. "I can't think why. Perhaps Crystal Point is a little tame for him." The words came out, but she wasn't sure from where.

Callie smiled. "I don't think Scott's looking for any kind of excitement while he's here. In fact, Crystal Point is probably exactly what he needs at the moment. Mike's death hit him pretty hard and after the inquest he probably should have taken some time out. But typically Scott, he went back to work straightaway."

Evie registered the other woman's words. "Mike?" was all she could get out of her mouth.

"They were friends," Callie explained. "And they worked together. I thought Scott might have told you." She pushed herself off the bench and crossed her arms. "You're easy to talk to, Evie—I'd hoped he might have opened up a bit."

Yes, usually she was easy to talk to. "Well, it's only been a few days," she said. "And we haven't spent a lot of time together." *Liar.* "Some people aren't comfortable talking with strangers."

Callie touched her arm. "You're not a stranger, Evie. You're the warmest, most genuine woman I've ever met."

"Thanks," she said, and tried to steer her thoughts away from Scott, and failed miserably. "Perhaps he's not ready to talk about it?'

Callie nodded. "Perhaps. You know, the other day, I thought…well, I thought that you and he looked kind of *close*." Her friend sighed. "I know it's silly of me. And I don't know why I thought I had any business thinking about it. I just did."

"Well, he's your brother," Evie said gently, not daring

to disclose anything. "And we all get a little protective of our brothers at times."

"Like you did," Callie reminded her. "When you asked me how I felt about Noah."

"That seems like forever ago now." She grabbed Callie's hand and touched the bright diamond glittering on her finger. "And look how good it turned out."

Evie stared at the ring. She'd taken her own wedding band off years ago. But she missed it. She missed the idea of truly belonging to someone, and having that someone belong to her. And she didn't quite realize how much up until days ago. Up until Scott had entered her life, her world. For years she'd been in a kind of emotional hibernation, safe from wanting anything. Safe from really *feeling* anything.

Her mother returned then and quickly ushered them both from the kitchen. Evie discarded the apron and followed Callie outside. The huge patio was filled with people, and typically her mother was the consummate hostess. Two long tables were covered with starchy white cloths and held trays of canapés and bite-size morsels of food. Evie helped herself to a glass of wine from the bar and mingled for a while.

It didn't take her long to head for the games room on the other side of the patio. The pool game was in full swing and she found a spot near the door to observe the players. Only, the moment Evie saw Scott leaning against a wall with a pool cue in his hand while he waited for his turn to shoot, he was all she noticed. The room was noisy, but she didn't hear any of it. It was as if the crowd parted of its own will, urging her to make eye contact with him. He looked back, tilted his head fractionally and almost smiled. Almost, because he stopped himself, she was sure of it. It gave her a strange feeling in her chest and she turned away after a few moments, grateful she was by the door for a quick escape.

Evie headed for the pool area. She could be alone there. She could think. She made her way through the gate and closed it securely behind herself. The terraced area behind the pool was usually reserved as a dance floor when her parents had parties, but thankfully it looked as though there would be no dancing tonight. She sat on one of the bench seats and placed her drink on the timber decking.

She heard the gate click and knew she had company. Without even seeing him she felt Scott's presence as if it pulsed through her. He didn't sit at first. He stood about six feet from her, cradling what looked to be an untouched beer in one hand. The underwater lights created an inviting mood.

"Did you abandon your game?" she asked, not as steadily as she would have liked.

He shrugged and sat down beside her, stretching out his long legs. "I'll let your brother and your policeman friend fight over who's the reigning alpha male in the group. I beat them twice and figured that was enough."

"Callie said you want to leave Dunn Inn?" she asked, figuring there was little point in avoiding the topic.

"I'm considering it."

Evie's belly dipped in an all-too-familiar way. He had the most mesmerizing effect on her. She breathed a soft "Why?" and waited for his reply.

Scott felt her looking at him, felt those incredible green eyes waiting for a response. "You know why."

She didn't say anything for a moment, and when she replied he thought she sounded a little breathless. "Because we're…because…"

"Because being around you makes it difficult not being with you."

He heard her breath catch in her throat. "Oh…well… even if that's the case, I'd still like you to stay. You know, to avoid any questions from the family."

Scott knew that. He'd known it even before the words left her beautiful mouth.

"Callie told me about your friend who died."

Did she, now? "Callie shouldn't have said anything to you."

"Don't be mad at her. She's concerned about you."

"I'm fine," he said, feeling the furthest thing from fine. "It was months ago."

"Why was there an inquest into his death?"

Callie *had* been busy. "Because he died on the job," Scott replied, feeling the words like they were glass in his mouth. "It's standard practice."

"Were you involved?"

It was the kind of question Scott would normally have fielded with an effective *none of your damned business*. But he couldn't say that to Evie. "I was there," he admitted. "We'd been called out to a house fire in Orange County. We knew it was gonna be bad because the smoke was thick and black. When we got there the place was well alight."

He stopped speaking and she half turned. "What happened?" she prompted.

Scott filled his lungs with air. "Mike was working an extra shift. Looking back, I knew he was tired, knew he should've gone home. But he had a family, a mortgage he was trying to stay on top of. When we found out what street the fire was on, I could see him getting agitated. He kept saying, "No way, no way." I didn't get what he meant at first and he didn't tell me. We were the second squad to get there. Mike started yelling, screaming something about getting the kids out. There were balloons tied to the mailbox and they started popping with the heat and it became pretty obvious there was a birthday party going on at the house."

A house full of kids, he thought, as memories leached through him. Actually a backyard full of kids, all screaming, and a set of parents trying to get the children to calm down and climb over the rear fence. None of which was working very well.

"Mike kept yelling, 'Where's Isabel, where's Isabel?'— his daughter," Scott explained when he saw Evie's expression. "*His* kid was at the party. And it was pretty obvious the fire would take the house—there was no saving it."

Even in the dim light Scott could see the sudden gray pallor on Evie's face. "And the children?"

"We got a vague head count from the supervising parents," he replied. "Some were in the front yard. Some had made it to the back fence and were being helped over by a neighbor."

"And Isabel?"

He shrugged, remembering the anguish on Mike's face as he searched for his daughter. "We were told a couple of the kids could be missing."

"Were they in the house?"

"We didn't know anything for sure. But Mike was certain she had to be inside and I couldn't make him think otherwise. And he said he was going in." It had been the worst possible scenario. Made even more so when he knew his friend was about to abandon all the training he'd had as a firefighter. "Mike headed inside. We knew it wasn't safe. The whole house was engulfed by this stage and two units were working on putting the flames out. And we had no proof that anyone was inside. I tried to talk him out of it, to make him realize the risk he was taking."

"He wouldn't listen?"

"No."

Evie touched his arm. "Did you go after him?"

"No."

Her grip tightened. "Did you want to?"

Scott's chest tightened. "Of course."

"But?"

He took a breath, letting it out quickly because he felt as if his lungs would explode. "But I had to ascertain the level of danger before I could allow myself or any of the crew to go into that building. So I made the call—I did my job—and I concluded that it was too dangerous. If I'd allowed anyone to go inside, another would have followed, and then another. I couldn't risk it. I wouldn't."

"So he went inside and didn't come out?"

"That's right."

"And his daughter?" she asked.

"Safe," he replied flatly. "But now without her father. She'd been safe all along in the neighbors' yard. Which is where I told Mike she would probably be."

Evie sighed. "It's impossible to reason with a distraught parent. I don't imagine anything you said would have made much difference."

"No," he agreed. "But I still…"

"Wonder if you should have done things differently?"

Could she read his mind? "Yeah, I guess I do. I was trained to react a certain way, to respond to situations by working toward the safest possible outcome. To save lives and property is the code a firefighter lives by," he said, feeling the gentle stroke of Evie's fingers against his arm and vaguely wondering why *her* touch gave him the kind of comfort he so often longed for. "But not at the expense of breaking ranks, or protocol—that's what we're taught from day one. People die when rules aren't followed."

She drew in a quick breath and he knew he'd struck a chord. "Yes, they do."

"So, maybe in my head I know I did the right thing—and the inquest confirmed that. But sometimes, when I think about his wife and daughters, I just wonder, what if I'd gone after him? Maybe he wouldn't have gotten so deep into the house before I could talk him around."

"You might have been killed, too."

He shrugged. "Perhaps. Or I might have been able to save him if I'd relied on my instincts rather than the rules."

"Aren't the rules there to keep you safe?" she asked, the soft voice of reason.

"Try telling that to Mike's wife." He sat back, careful not to move his arm in case she released him. For now, Scott was content to feel her soft touch. "He had a chance for a desk job. He wouldn't take it. He thought he'd be selling out. It was better hours and better suited to a man in his position."

"You mean a man with a wife and children?"

"Yeah."

She took a moment to respond. "You make it sound like someone without a family is more expendable."

"Not expendable exactly. Just with fewer people to leave behind."

"I'm sure your mother and sister wouldn't think so," she said softly. "Or anyone else who...who cares about you."

He wondered for a moment if she was one of those people, and then felt stupid because they hardly knew each other. But she was still touching him, still rubbing his arm in that slow burning way which was not quite seductive, but not exactly platonic, either. "I guess that puts me in my place, then." He felt her smile through to the blood in his veins. He looked at her hand. "If you keep doing that, Evie, I'm going to forget all about my good intentions."

She removed her hand immediately. "Sorry," she said.

"Habit. I'm a touchy kind of person. I obviously need to set some boundaries."

Scott didn't like the sound of that. The last thing he wanted was a wall between them. He wanted her so much he could barely function. And she looked so beautiful in her green dress and silver sandals.

"Don't apologize," he said. "I liked it."

She looked directly ahead and spoke in a quiet voice. "Is your friend's death the reason why you think relationships and the job don't mix?"

Scott didn't bother to deny it. "I saw what Mike went through, trying to juggle the two and he never seemed to have much of a handle on either. He told me once he didn't think he was a great father or husband— and sometimes his mind wasn't on the job." Scott wished she'd touch him again, or wished he had the courage to touch her. "You know, there have been times when I've arrived at a fire and thought—this one looks bad, so is this it? But I still go in—I go in knowing I have to, I go in knowing being a firefighter is all I've ever wanted to do. Mike was like that, too, once. But he got married and had a couple of kids and he changed—he took shortcuts, he improvised, he made mistakes because he was distracted. You can't afford to do that in this job. If you do you may end up paying the ultimate price. As Mike did."

Scott felt as if a valve inside him had been released. He'd kept those thoughts to himself for eight months. And he held strong in his convictions.

"I understand what you're saying, but I'm not sure I agree with you."

He'd wondered if she would. And he respected her opinion. So he asked her a blunt question. "Do you think your husband's mind was on the job that night he went out?"

Evie's head snapped around. She went to say something,

but stopped. And she looked at him for the longest time. Finally, she spoke. "No, I don't imagine it was."

"Because he would have been thinking about everything he hadn't done at home. He would have been thinking about the approaching storm and wondering if you were okay. As well trained as he was, as prepared as he was, those distractions might have cost him his life."

Scott saw her stiffen. "I hope I was more than a distraction to my husband."

He'd offended her. He was an idiot. "I apologize—that didn't come out right. I can be clumsy when I'm nervous."

"Nervous?" she echoed, as though she couldn't believe it. "Of what?"

Scott managed a smile. "You," he admitted. "Being within touching distance of a beautiful woman makes every man nervous."

"I'm not beautiful," she protested. "Now, my sister Grace, she's beautiful."

"I didn't notice," he replied, and wondered how she'd not know she was the most beautiful woman on the planet. *Man, I've got it bad. I should pack my stuff and get away from Crystal Point as fast as I can. Clumsy* wasn't the word for how he felt at the moment. *Hotly aroused* was more like it. "Maybe we should get back to the party?"

Evie nodded. "Yes, good idea." She stood up and he followed. Before they reached the pool gate she stopped. "You know," she said firmly, leaning toward him just a fraction. "Your friend…he wanted to save his child." She took a breath, coming closer. "And until you're a father yourself, I don't think you should criticize his motivations. It might be okay to have your principles set in stone if you've got experience to back them up—if you don't, you just end up looking like an immature, judgmental ass."

With that, she turned on her sandals and walked from the pool area.

Scott remained where he was and stared after her. And he smiled. Evie Dunn had his number. And at that moment he wanted her more than he'd ever wanted anyone or anything in his life.

Chapter Seven

On Sunday night Evie took in a movie with Fiona. The few hours away from the inn gave her a chance to think. About herself. About Trevor. And about Scott. Thoughts of her outburst by the pool at her parents' house lingered in her thoughts. Lectures were not usually her thing.

When she returned home the lights were still on downstairs and she headed for the living room to say good-night to her guests before going to bed. Only her guests were in the dining room, scattered around the big table, playing rummy. And Scott sat at the head, dealing the cards.

"Come and join us?" Flora suggested.

But Evie was not in the mood for games. She wanted to climb into bed and go to sleep. She wanted to forget about how all she'd thought about during the romantic chick-flick was locking lips with Scott. And looking at him didn't help. He wore a white T-shirt, and the soft fabric molded to his perfectly and sinfully sculptured chest. The Kellers were holding hands at one end of the table, the Manning sisters were giving their cards serious attention and Scott was watching her with blistering intensity.

"Wh-where's Trevor?" she asked shakily.

"Bed."

Heat traveled up her back like a serpent. The very word conjured up a whole lot of images she tried desperately to ignore. "Oh, well…I think I'll—"

A chair moved and she realized he'd pushed it out with his foot. "He's a little old to need tucking in, right?" Scott gestured to the chair. "Come and sit down."

No exactly an order, but pretty close. Evie fought the stab of resentment behind her ribs and faked a smile. No scenes in front of her paying guests. Just smiles and a happy face. Right, she could do that. She sat down and took the cards Scott dealt her. She got a lousy hand and wondered if he'd done it deliberately. Then she figured someone so unyielding wouldn't consider cheating. His mouth twisted fractionally, as if he knew, and that set a determined pulse through Evie's blood. Evie was a master at rummy. She'd beat his pants off. Well, maybe not his pants—although the idea of strip rummy seemed scandalously erotic. If they were alone. Which they weren't. And if she had any intention of setting her inhibitions free. Which she didn't. So she needed to forget all about that in a hurry.

She lost the first round, won the second and third and was hyped up to make it three in a row when the Kellers and Amelia announced they'd had enough. Once the cards were packed away, the chairs pushed in and the few empty glasses placed on the sideboard, everyone said good-night and moved toward the wide doorway.

Except Patti Keller gave a delighted shriek and said, "Mistletoe!"

Evie stopped dead in her tracks. And looked up. And

nearly choked. Sure enough, there is was. Directly above her. And directly above Scott.

No way.

Four pairs of curious eyes looked straight at her. And Evie knew exactly what their look meant. She also wasn't having anything to do with it.

"It's tradition," Flora said, and both of her silver brows rose. "I thought you were a stickler for it?"

She was—usually. But not when faced with the idea of kissing Scott Jones in front of a roomful of people. Okay, maybe not a room *full*—but there was enough of an audience to rattle her usual ramrod composure. She had no intention of doing anything so ludicrous. Especially when she felt as if she'd been set up. When she *knew* she'd been set up. And the two gray-haired old ladies in front of her didn't seem to have the need to hide the fact. She looked at Scott, saw his amused, almost I-dare-you-to grin and wanted the floor to open up and suck her in.

"We'll go first," Patti announced, and promptly dragged her bewildered-looking husband beneath the doorway and kissed him.

Newlyweds, Evie thought with an inward groan. She'd seen dozens of them come through Dunn Inn. All of them had possessed that same look as Patti Keller—that dreamy, I-can't-wait-to-get-my-hands-on-my-man look. *Was I ever like that?* She couldn't remember. Had Gordon's kisses knocked her off her feet? Had she let him? Had she been so immersed in her role as the sensible Preston daughter she'd forgotten to live a passionate life?

Passion…the idea of it teased around the edges of her thoughts. And sex, well, that was supposed to be passionate, wasn't it? She considered her options—the Kellers were still kissing, the Manning sisters were waiting and Scott hadn't moved an inch.

So she ditched her sensible garb for a few moments, swiveled on her heel, stood on her toes and kissed Scott Jones. Just like that. Evie could feel him smiling beneath the soft pressure of her mouth. Her body thrummed, her blood sang in her veins. Kissing Scott was like nothing on earth.

When she was done she pulled away, stepped back and flashed a kind of is-everyone-happy-now? smile.

Then she waltzed from the room without another word.

Scott had always thought he knew himself. He knew what he wanted, where he was going, where he'd been. Granted, Mike's death had shaken up his world and made him question his skills as a firefighter. But this was something else.

Evie...

He could still taste the sweet softness of her lips when she'd kissed him underneath the mistletoe. His attraction for her was consuming his thoughts. Like now, while they were in the car on their way back from Noah and Callie's. They'd gone to her brother's home for dinner and it was the first time they'd been alone for two days.

"You're very quiet."

She let out a breath. "I'm just thinking."

So was he. About kissing Evie. About the scent of her perfume. About how he couldn't get her out of his head. About how she was the most remarkable woman he'd ever met. "What about?"

"Trevor," she said softly. "I was thinking about my son."

Scott laughed silently at his own self-indulgent conceit that she might have been thinking about him. She had a son and she sounded concerned. "Is there a problem?"

"No, not really."

"But?" he asked as he turned onto the bitumen road.

"I was watching Noah with his kids," she replied, settling her arms around her waist. "It got me thinking about how Trevor must miss his dad."

Suddenly it got Scott thinking, too. He remembered the conversation he'd had with Trevor when they'd shot hoops together. "Natural he'd miss him. But he had a good father, right?"

"The operative word being *had*." The pain on her face was evident.

"He has you," Scott said gently.

She looked at him and Scott stole a sideways glance. "He's a lot like his dad."

"He's like *you*."

She smiled. "I guess in some ways. But I watched my brother with his son tonight and saw what an incredible relationship that was and wondered if I'd been…selfish."

Scott glanced at her. "Why would you think that?"

Her beautiful hair rustled. "Because…I haven't married again."

Married. He wasn't sure why the idea twisted at his insides. "You can only live the life you're meant to live, Evie," he said, and then thought he'd made no sense at all.

But she nodded as though she understood. "Maybe. Only, Trevor *should* have had a father…and I… The truth is I shut down after Gordon died. I guess I shut down so much I didn't think about what Trevor might need. I just decided that to be the best parent I could be I had to give my son *all* of me. And it made it easier, too," she admitted. "I didn't have to consider what it might do to us if I brought someone else into our life. But maybe I let him down by not…well, at least I could have considered it."

"If that's what you want…you should," he said, though the words felt like rocks in his mouth. The thought of Evie with another man made it actually hurt behind his ribs.

But he was right to say it—right to get the words out between them. He was leaving in two weeks and in no shape to offer her anything other than sex. And Evie deserved way more than that. As much as part of him wanted her more than he could remember wanting anything in his life. "Even an immature, judgmental ass like me can see that."

He turned the car into the driveway and braked outside the studio.

She twisted in her seat when the car came to a halt. "I'm sorry about that. I didn't mean to come across all bossy and patronizing."

Scott smiled and killed the engine. "Sure you did."

She smiled back. "Well, maybe. But I shouldn't have. I sometimes forget that I don't have all the answers. You came here for your sister's wedding, not lectures from someone who wouldn't have a clue what it must be like to put your life on the line every day."

"Apology accepted," he said. "Though I probably deserved it."

"Perhaps a little," she said, and smiled. "And about before…what I said about Trevor. I'm not complaining…not really…it's only that sometimes," she said, suddenly seeming incredibly young and vulnerable. "I feel like I'm stuck in this role of being a certain kind of person. A certain kind of woman. And as that woman I always do what's expected, what's the right thing. I get this sense that being… I don't know…suffocated almost…as if I've suffocated myself by being *who* I am. I've built this orderly, safe life which at times feels like a jail cell."

Scott's heart thundered beneath his ribs. "And what, Evie? You want to break out?"

She shrugged a little. "I think about it. I think what it might be like to be…I don't know…different."

Heat filled the space between them, flicking into life,

energizing the air with its tiny atoms. Even in the dim light Scott could see the brightness of her eyes, the way her lips parted slightly, as though she was about to say something, as though she wanted to…to… He shook the feeling off, knowing he was nuts to keep thinking about her in that way. But he wanted to kiss her so much. He wanted to feel the skin on her shoulders beneath his hands, he wanted to taste the delicate spot behind her ear and then go lower, past her throat and lower still, to breasts he knew, without ever having touched them, ever having had them pressed naked against him, were glorious and round and sensitive and made for his hands and mouth. He wanted to kiss her ribs, her belly, her thighs… He want to bury his mind, his body, in the softness of her skin. He was more aroused than he could ever remember being in his life, and she hadn't even touched him!

"You better make a run for it," he said, more groan than words.

She obviously heard him, but remained where she was, drawing in breath. "I should, yes."

Scott inhaled deeply and the scent of her ripped through his blood. If he moved a few inches she would be in his arms. And she wouldn't resist—he felt that with mind-blowing certainty. "Last chance."

She turned, easing toward him. Scott raised one hand and touched her cheek. He didn't imagine the way her lips parted, or the way her tongue rested on her white teeth. The need to kiss her, possess her surged across his skin. And he didn't have to wait. She came willingly, moving her body across the space dividing them and pressed her mouth to his. Scott responded instantly, taking her lips in a searing kiss that rocked him to the very core. His hands moved to her shoulders and he molded the delicate bones beneath his palms. The kiss went on, drugging, hot, kicking at his libido like a jackhammer. She moaned low in her throat as he cupped the underswell of her breast. Heat radiated through the T-shirt she wore and Scott felt her nipple peak against his thumb.

I haven't made out in a car since I was a teenager.

And I shouldn't be doing it with a woman like Evie.

The realization was like a bucket of cold water.

"Evie," he said hoarsely. "We should stop. This isn't the place—"

She wrenched free as he spoke. "You're right," she said, and pulled herself into a sitting position. She grabbed the door handle and pushed herself out of the car. He watched her race toward the house, her incredible hips swinging in her jeans. Within seconds she'd opened the front door and disappeared into the house. He stayed where he was, willing his body to play fair and return to normal.

It took a while. And it gave him a chance to think. The struggle to ignore his feelings for Evie was getting more and more difficult.

It's getting damn well impossible.

He didn't want them. Or need them. Feelings only blurred his focus. And lack of focus in his line of work could prove deadly. He'd seen evidence of that firsthand. Mike had lost his edge. Scott wasn't about to make the same mistake. Every instinct he had told him to back off from Evie. He couldn't do serious, and she deserved better.

I will not get involved.

And I really should have moved to a hotel.

Evie canceled her usual Thursday night dinner for her guests. The Kellers had left that morning and the Manning sisters were visiting a niece in Bellandale and wouldn't be back until late. She had new guests arriving the following day and needed to get the Kellers' room cleaned and prepared.

Although nothing helped stop her thinking about Scott.

I would have made love with him last night.

No doubt about it. She would have thrown off every part of herself that she'd trained to do the right thing, the sensible thing, and gone to wherever he might have taken her.

Her body screamed for the kind of release she sensed instinctively he would give her. Sex hadn't seemed so important for the longest time. And she wondered why, beyond his obvious physical appeal, that it was Scott who'd pulled her from her sexless haze. After so long, after Gordon...it didn't make sense. She wasn't the casual sex type. Making love had always been exactly that. And with her husband she'd been in the security of a loving relationship. She'd met and fallen in love with Gordon in high school, and exploring her sexuality with him had been safe.

But this feeling she had for Scott...it was *all* risk.

In the car she'd felt the burn of his possession like a brand on her skin. His kisses drove her wild. His touch sent her body to another place. And knowing that it was mutual, knowing that he'd been as turned on as she'd been, made the moment all the more potent.

Evie also knew she had to resist whatever feelings were running riot inside her.

Baring all her thoughts and feelings about her son wasn't exactly helping her cause, either. She never bared her soul. She never really let anyone in. At least, not since Gordon.

But Scott had her running on both fronts—her body and her heart. She just wasn't sure which one would give out first.

* * *

On Friday evening Evie ditched her regular class and headed for the local elementary school to watch her brother's three youngest children perform in the annual Christmas play. She hadn't seen Scott much at all over the past couple of days. She'd kept herself busy in her studio or with her guests. She often heard Scott shooting hoops with Trevor, and her son had even taken up running with Scott for the past couple of mornings.

She wasn't sure what Scott did with himself during the day and didn't have the courage to ask. And he usually returned to Dunn Inn well after dinner had been served and retired straight to his room. Their earlier routine of a late coffee and conversation had disappeared as quickly as it had begun.

Trevor had declined to attend the concert and she let her son have his way. He was spending the night at his best friend's house, where no doubt the boys would be playing video games until the small hours of the morning.

A special stage and seating had been set up on the sports field, and Evie weaved her way through the crowds, looking for her brother and Callie. Instead, she found Scott.

Callie and Noah were seated beside him and for a few extraordinary seconds he held her complete attention. The dip in her belly, the way her heart raced…what had once been long forgotten and unfamiliar feelings were now all *too* familiar.

Feelings she had no idea what to do with.

Evie hung back and walked around the rear of the seating area. The music started and a group of children dressed in variations of red and green elf costumes came onto the stage and broke into delightful versions of "Santa Claus is Coming to Town" and "Frosty the Snowman." The singing made her smile, especially when she spotted her eight-year-old nephew, Jamie, in the exuberant group. When the song changed to "Jingle Bells" several younger children joined the choir onstage and Noah's twins were among them. She looked back toward her brother. He and Callie were watching the kids with obvious pride and enjoyment. And there was a vacant seat beside them.

"Can we talk?"

She stilled. Scott was directly behind her. So close she felt the warmth coming off his skin. Evie didn't turn around. "Sure," she said in a wobbly voice. "Later. At home."

"Now, Evie," he insisted.

The music volume rose and she tilted back a little and collided with his chest. It would have been easier to refuse him. Better even. But she didn't. "Okay," she said, and stepped away.

Evie knew the school grounds well. She'd attended as a youngster, as had her son, and she still volunteered at the canteen once a week. She walked through the mill of people hanging behind the seating and headed for the old library building. The sound of children singing faded substantially once she rounded the corner with Scott in her wake. It was quiet and private and had some light courtesy of an open window from a nearby classroom. Evie turned by the steps and thrust her hands to her hips.

"So…what?"

He looked her up and down. "I'm moving out."

No great surprise. She'd sensed it from his conspicuous absence over the past couple of days.

"When?"

"Tomorrow."

So soon. It took Evie about two seconds to work out that she didn't want Scott to go anywhere. "Trevor will be disappointed." *Trevor?* She wondered why she'd said

hat. Wondered where it came from. Guilt trips weren't
ner scene. She shrugged casually. "I mean, he'll be disappointed you won't be around to help improve his basketball technique."

"And you?"

Evie stepped back and leaned against the steel stair rail.
"I don't…I don't have any claim on you."

He moved forward. The jeans and black T-shirt he wore
did little to disguise his infinite attributes, and her mouth
turned dry. "I'm not so sure about that, Evie," he said as
he reached for her and she melted against him. "Right
now, at this moment…I'd say you've got more claim than
anyone else."

It was a highly provocative thing to say and Evie felt
the meaning through to her bones. She also felt him…
His strong, lean body and wide shoulders. With his arms
around her Evie had a faraway, drifting thought that she'd
never felt so safe in all her life.

Scott kissed her thoroughly and she kissed him right
back. Evie curved her hands over his shoulders as he pulled
her close and the kissing continued. So did the soft stroke
of his fingertips up and down her spine. She felt the heat of
his touch through the fabric of her black dress and moaned
low in her throat. Her fingers moved over his shoulders,
drawing them closer, and Scott curved a hand down her
hip and lower. When his fingertips touched her thigh and
drew her skirt higher, Evie gasped against his mouth.

There was a vague sound of carols in the background
and the echo of laughter and applause. Thankfully, it pulled
her from the seductive trance long enough to come to her
senses. She pulled back and drew in a shuddering breath.
"Stop…please."

Scott released her and she stepped back, breathing hard.
He didn't look any better off.

"I'm sorry," he said, and crossed his arms tightly. "I shouldn't have done that."

They both shouldn't have. Out in the open, where they could be seen. At a school, no less. She wished Sensible Evie would come back. Before she had a chance to say anything, he turned on his heel and walked off, disappearing into the darkness.

She should have stayed and watched the rest of the performance, should have shared the small piece of Christmas spirit with her family. But Evie was in no mood to put on fake smiles and pretend she had it all together. Fifteen minutes later she was home and upstairs, pacing the space between the sitting room and small kitchenette. She flicked on a table lamp and sat on the sofa for a while, shifting position every time she heard a car pass outside. Half an hour had inched by when she finally heard the distinctive sound of Scott's motorcycle pulling up in the driveway, and her heart almost landed in her throat. She heard the downstairs door open, heard the steady thud of his feet on the stairs as he climbed them.

He came through the doorway and made a jerky stop. He looked her up and down, taking in the short dress and low heels, and she watched as he swallowed hard. An uneasy silence fell between them. And for the first time in the longest time, Evie knew exactly what she wanted. *And who.* Even if it was only for one night. She drew in a deep breath and spoke.

"Part of me wishes I could stop wanting you," she admitted, and bit down on her lip. "Part of me wishes you'd never come here."

He didn't move. "And the other part?"

Evie shrugged, half hopeless, half confused. "I've done the right thing all my life. I've always put everyone else's needs first. I've never jumped into anything without thinking about it. And as a woman, I haven't let myself really *feel* anything for such a long time." Another breath came out. "Ten years," she said on a sigh. "I haven't…I haven't…well, since my husband died…there's not been anyone else."

He didn't say a word. He simply stared at her with such hot, blistering intensity it was as though for that moment, they were the only two people on the planet. Evie met his look head-on and felt the vibration of him directly though to her bones, and deeper, to that place where she never imagined she'd feel anything again after her husband died.

Finally, he spoke. "What do you want to happen between us, Evie?"

She drew in a long breath. "I want…I want you to make love to me."

Chapter Eight

Scott knew he had to keep his head. This wasn't a one-night-stand kind of woman. This was Evie. And as much as he ached for her, he suspected that once they became lovers, leaving her would be like losing a limb.

"You know that making love will complicate things," he said quietly. "Sex *always* complicates things."

"I know," she admitted. "And I don't expect promises or declarations of any kind. We're two very different people with different lives. But this *thing* between us is stronger than I am."

It was stronger than him, too. He'd spent the past week in a haze, knowing he probably shouldn't want her, knowing it would only ever be temporary. But he longed for Evie in ways he'd never longed for any woman before.

"What if sex turns into something else…something more?"

She moved her legs. "It won't. We'll make sure it won't.

Look, I'm not denying that I like you. I do. But we both know anything serious isn't viable."

It sounded like every man's dream. Sex with a beautiful woman and no strings attached. Only, his dreams suddenly felt as if they were shifting, morphing into something he couldn't quite figure. "So, you want to have an affair?" It sounded old-fashioned, put like that. But he wasn't sure what to call it.

She nodded. "Yes. For as long as it lasts," she said.

For as long as you are here. That's what she meant. "And no commitment?"

"That's right." Her eyes suddenly looked huge in her face. "I don't want you to think I'm looking for... Well, the other night I said some things about my son, about how I should have remarried. This isn't about *that*," she said pointedly. "I've no illusions, Scott, and you've made it pretty clear you're not in any kind of position to be anyone's...husband. And I'm not in a position to believe in fairy tales. This is what it is and I'm okay with that."

Scott's heartbeat was erratic. He wanted her so much. *And here she is, asking me to make love to her.* But she hadn't been with anyone for ten years. To be her first lover since her husband had died suddenly seemed a huge responsibility. A big deal. And certainly worthy of more than just an affair. But to refuse her? When his body, his mind, was screaming to possess every part of the woman she was.

I could walk away right now...I could walk away and not know how it feels to touch her and love her and wake up beside her in the morning.

But he didn't walk.

"Evie," he said softly. "Come here."

By the time she reached him Scott's hands were burning to touch her. The simple black dress she wore was sleeveless and her shoulders were enticingly smooth, her arms supple and sun kissed. But it was her face that held him captive. As it had from the first moment they'd met. He'd never met anyone with lips like hers. Or such wide green eyes and provocative slanting brows.

"You're staring at me," she said when they stood no more than a foot apart.

"I can't help it," he admitted, and looked at her hair hanging loose down her back. He reached out and twirled a few strands between his fingers. "You have the most amazing hair."

She half smiled. "My one beauty."

"Hardly," he said, and continued to play with her curls.

He touched the back of her neck and drew her closer. Finally, he felt her against him, felt the soft curves of her hips and breasts against his stomach and chest. Scott looked down into her face and titled her head backward. He heard her suck in a shallow breath, felt the slight tremble of her body and instinctively drew his arm around her, settling his hand at her waist. He took his time to kiss her, knowing how her mouth would taste, but wanting to savor the feeling. Evie's hands came to his shoulders and she clung to him as their lips met. She groaned low in her throat, half resistance, half insistence, and he deepened the kiss, tracing the outline of her mouth with his tongue. When her tongue touched his Scott almost jumped out of his skin.

"Your bedroom," she muttered against his lips.

He didn't waste time thinking why she'd prefer his room to hers. He kissed her again, hungrier, deeper, before he grasped her hand and led her down the hall.

"Are you sure about this, Evie?" he asked once they were in his room. "If at any point you want to stop, just say the word and I'll—"

"Do you always talk this much before you take a woman

to bed?" she asked, flicking the lock on the door and bridging the gap between them.

Scott smiled. "Not usually. I told you I get clumsy when I'm nervous."

She placed her hands on his chest. "You're nervous about having sex with me?"

"Not exactly," he said, fighting the ever-increasing surge of arousal just being near her wreaked on his body. "You've waited a long time… I just want to be…worthy."

"Do you want me to rate your performance out of ten? If you like I'll take—"

"Now who's talking too much?" he said, and reached for her.

As kisses went, the next one didn't have a whole lot of finesse, but he made his point, because she stopped talking and just kissed him back. And then again, and again. He couldn't get enough of the taste of her or the feel of her tongue curling around his own. Her hands were at the hem of his T-shirt and she gently tugged at it. It made Scott smile and he quickly pulled the shirt over his head.

When she touched his skin Scott felt the heat in her fingertips. He let her decide the pace their lovemaking would take, and for the moment she seemed perfectly content to simply touch his chest and shoulders. Of course, he was burning to touch her, too, but he held back and clenched his fists as tightly as he could. She had a soft touch, not quite tentative, but…exploring. He liked that about her— liked that she was patient and wasn't all rush and haste.

When she was done she rested her hands on his belly and traced his abdominals with her fingers. The sensation was so powerful Scott felt as though all the blood in his body had surged to his groin. She looked up at him and smiled. "Your turn."

He liked that about her, too. She wasn't all serious and

tense about touching him. He didn't want serious between them. Her fingers inched a little lower and Scott sucked in a breath. His arms came around her and he slowly undid the zipper on the dress. It slipped down her shoulders and over her hips with a quiet swoosh and landed at her feet. She wore black lace briefs that were quite modest but sexy as hell and hit his libido with the precision of an arrow.

"You are sensational," he said in a hoarse whisper.

She smiled again and stepped back, flipping the dress aside with her foot before she discarded her heels. Scott drank in the sheer magnitude of her sexy, mind-blowing beauty. Her breasts tilted upward in the half-cup bra and his palms itched to touch them. Her waist and stomach and the curvy flare of her hips were enough to fulfill his every fantasy.

Evie walked around him to flick on the bedside light and he got a great view of her toned, shapely behind. She walked back to the door and turned off the main light. It undid him, looking at her like that, watching her move around the room in her underwear.

Scott gripped her fingers and led Evie to the big bed in the center of the room. She backed her knees against the mattress and reached for the snap on his jeans. He was hard and ready for her and she knew it. She brushed her hand across the abrasive denim, feeling his erection, and he knew if he didn't start loving her soon, if he didn't get inside her soon, he might die a slow death.

He molded her shoulders with his hands and crooked his fingers beneath her bra strap. She was looking at him, smiling, waiting. Scott moved lower and cupped her breasts. Her nipples were already hard, jutting against the stretchy lace, and he traced them with his fingertips. She groaned low in her throat, and the sound pierced through him. He reached around her back with one hand and unclipped her bra with one deft flick. Once her breasts were free, Scott bent his head and closed his mouth over one rosy nipple, and as he sucked the peak she groaned again and threaded her fingers through his hair.

When he came back up to look at her, Scott was so turned on he feared his legs might give way. He gently coaxed her onto the bed, kissing her shoulder, her neck and her bountiful breasts. She undid his jeans and Scott sucked in a breath and took about three seconds to remove the rest of his clothes. He kissed her, over and over, everywhere, anywhere, light kisses, slow kisses, and pushed her briefs off in one movement.

And then he touched her center, parting the soft curls as he inched his finger inside her. Slowly, so excruciatingly slow, she pushed her hips forward. But Scott had no intention of rushing anything. Not with Evie. She was a woman who deserved to be loved right. And she'd chosen him to love her…even if only for one night. And he would make it good for her, despite the aching hunger he felt to be inside her and stay there until they didn't know when he began and she ended. She was wet and hot and he teased the tender flesh with his thumb. She rocked against him and he found the pressure she liked, sliding his hand over her, gently rubbing the slick nub he'd found with his finger. He kissed her breasts and licked each tightly beaded nipple while he explored the heart of her and heard her breathing change as she came apart in his arms.

Watching her climax, feeling her shudder against him and say his name, was so sweetly consuming, that Scott experienced an unheralded tightness behind his eyes. He gave her a moment, pushing her hair from her face as she came back to earth.

She said something as she pressed her mouth to his chest and he caught the muffled words. "Absolutely," he said quickly, twisted one arm around to rummage in the bedside drawer with eager fingers.

"That sure of me?" she asked, tracing hot kisses down his belly.

Scott grasped her chin and urged her to look at him. "Not really."

She smiled, took the foil packet and laid it on the bed and continued her exploration of his stomach and then lower still. Not shy, as he might have expected, but a sensual, confident woman who kissed and licked his skin.

"Evie," he groaned, and grasped her shoulders. "Evie," he said again, more plea than statement.

Without a word she grabbed the condom, ripped open the packet and slowly and torturously sheathed him. She scooted up and Scott took her in his arms, rolling her beneath him as he supported his weight on his elbows. Her thighs dropped against the mattress and he found her slowly, looking directly into her eyes as they joined. She gripped around him and he rocked against her, filling her so completely he thought he might pass out.

Have I ever felt like this before? Has anything ever felt this good...this right?

"Say something," she whispered.

"I...can't," he admitted raggedly, and began to move inside her.

In all her life, Evie had never felt so gloriously free, so totally uninhibited. Being with Scott, feeling the weight of his hard body and the heat of his possession, thrilled her in ways she hadn't imagined. She had no fear, no lingering concerns about her imperfections. The moment he'd looked at her in her sensible underwear and smiled that sexy smile all her remaining body image issues faded. Whatever happened after these precious moments she didn't care to know. She felt alive, desired, confident. She felt like a woman who'd met her match, who'd been in a state of sexual limbo only because she'd been waiting... for this night...this man.

She wrapped her arms around him and splayed her hands across his strong back, matching his movements so perfectly she wondered briefly about all her past notions of awkwardness and embarrassment when she'd imagined being with a lover after so many years of abstinence. There was none of that. Just two people who knew each other, somehow, who knew how to please, to pleasure, knew how to touch and stroke and give and take. And he felt wondrous—above her, against her, inside her, so much a part of her Evie wondered how she'd lived for so long without knowing such a feeling.

When the pleasure built again she went with it, matching his thrusts, his need. He kissed her as if he couldn't get enough of her taste or her tongue and she kissed him back eagerly, their mouths mimicking the act where their bodies joined. And she held on, clinging, urging and giving. And then it came, lifting her up, taking her so high she clung to his shoulders and let the sensation pulse through her body in a wave of pleasure so powerful she felt as if she'd transcended to another level of being. When he joined her in that place, Evie gripped him with all her strength, feeling his back tense, his body shudder and finally let go to be consumed by a powerful release.

He stayed where he was for a moment, drawing in long breaths. Evie could feel the furious beat of his heart pounding. His lips nuzzled her neck and she tenderly pushed his damp hair back from his forehead. After a couple of minutes he roused and shifted from her.

"I'll be back in a minute," he said as he swung off the bed and headed for the bathroom.

Evie stretched her limbs and closed her eyes. *Well, I've gone and done it now.* She lifted her knees up, pushed back the bedclothes and wiggled beneath the sheet. When Scott returned she was respectably covered and didn't linger to imagine why on earth she'd suddenly be shy about him seeing her naked, considering what they'd been doing for the past hour. He, on the other hand, didn't seem shy in the least, because he came around the bed, still in a state of semiarousal, and sat beside her.

He grasped both her hands and held them within his own. "Everything okay?"

"Of course."

"No regrets?"

"Not yet," she said honestly.

It made him smile a little. "Fair enough," he said, pulling the sheet back before Evie could protest, and looked her over with obvious admiration. He traced the back of his hand over her rib cage and then along the curve of her waist. Evie tried to grasp the sheet, but he pushed it back. "Don't do that."

Now the lovemaking was over, she could feel the fingers of reality grabbing at her. And for the first time since she'd entered his bedroom, she felt the burning scrutiny of his blue-eyed gaze.

"I'm not twenty anymore," she said pointedly.

Scott continued to touch her. "I'd be very disappointed if you were." His hand dipped lower, touching her intimately. "You have a lovely body."

"Flawed," she said, and thought how incredible his touch was as she gave him a very deliberate once over. "Unlike you."

He grinned, probably with more modesty than he felt, and it made Evie smile. So, the man had a perfect body? Didn't that simply make her the luckiest woman on the planet? She touched his chest and traced her fingertips downward toward his navel and the line of soft hair trailing down his faultlessly flat abdomen. When her hand came into contact with his very obvious erection, her libido did a wild leap. She wanted him again. And she knew he wanted her, too.

"Flawed?" His brows came together. "Are you kidding?" His hand moved across her thighs and then over her hips and belly. "This is beauty," he said, kissing the sensitive spot near her hip. "And this," he said, moving across, going lower, sliding his lips toward the juncture at her thighs.

And then neither of them said anything else for a long while.

Evie woke up alone. The clock on the bedside table flashed the time and she squinted to get a good look. Eight-forty? Impossible. She looked at light beaming through the crack in the curtains and shoved her face back into the pillow. She had to get up. There were guests to feed, things to be done. Guests who'd arrived yesterday and who would be wondering where she was, and if it wasn't for Amelia's and Flora's advancing years she was certain they'd crack it up the stairs to find out what had kept her from attending to her usual morning routine.

What kept me from it is nowhere to be seen.

Evie doubted Scott had gone for his usual morning run. She couldn't imagine he'd have the energy for anything after their night together. She certainly felt an aching lethargy in her limbs. Even her skin felt tired.

When the door opened about thirty seconds later and he walked into the room, she was appalled to see how chipper he looked, considering that she wanted to pull the sheet over her head and sleep for the remainder of the day. He was showered, dressed in cargos and a white polo shirt and looked completely recovered.

"Breakfast," he said, and Evie noticed the tray he carried.

Food sounded good, but she had to set her priorities. "I can't," she told him. "I have guests to—"

"All done," he said, and carried the tray to the bed. "Sit up a bit."

Evie jackknifed up immediately and clutched the sheet against her breasts. "What do you mean it's all done?"

"Well, I could hardly let your paying guests starve. And you were sleeping so soundly I didn't have the heart to wake you."

"You cooked breakfast?"

He shrugged and placed the small tray on the bedside table. "I made toast for Amelia and Flora," he replied with a smile. "I'm very talented."

She knew that. Her body had experienced firsthand his many talents. "What did you tell them?"

He held out a coffee mug. "That you were laid up in bed."

Evie struggled to keep the sheet in place. "Oh, God, what must they—"

"I said you were laid up," he said quickly, grinning. "Not getting laid."

Evie took the coffee, and the sheet fell to her waist. Scott looked immediately at her exposed breasts, and a flash of desire sparked in his eyes.

"I should still start moving," she said, took a sip of coffee and placed the mug on the tray before she shimmied off the bed.

He passed her one of his T-shirts to wear. "Let's go Christmas shopping."

Evie's eyes widened. Shopping? She took the shirt and quickly covered herself. "I'm not sure I—"

"I need to buy gifts for Callie's new family," he explained, and watched as she grabbed her clothes. "You know them better than I do. And I need to get something for my mom."

Christmas gift shopping? Why not? It didn't mean they were together. It didn't add to their one-night, no-strings agreement. And it would give her a chance to prove to herself that she was completely in control.

"Okay. Give me half an hour."

Evie rushed to shower and change into jeans and tank-style T-shirt and sandals. She wrote a note for Trevor, saying she would be in town for a few hours and back before lunch, then headed downstairs. Evie avoided the Manning sisters—certain they'd ask what she'd been up to and where she was going. She swung her tote across one shoulder and walked outside.

Scott was leaning against her car. "All set?"

Evie nodded and tossed him the keys. The drive into Bellandale took fifteen minutes and she gave him instructions directly to the larger of the two shopping malls in town. They parked underneath and headed up the elevator. Within the air-conditioned comfort of the mall, it was easy to forget about the rising humidity outside. While the Northern Hemisphere enjoyed the traditional cold weather, turkey and rich puddings, an Australian Christmas usually meant blistering heat, cold ham, shrimp and salads and icy beer. But Evie still got wrapped up in the festive season. She loved decorating her tree and buying gifts and settling in front of the television to watch *Miracle on 34th Street* with her son every year. She knew Trevor only tolerated the old black-and-white movie for her benefit and it made her love her son just that little bit more.

The mall was busy and shoppers were milling around retailers and freestanding stalls. There was a long queue of children waiting for a snapshot with Santa, and the charity gift wrap bar was in full swing.

"So," Scott said, and lightly grabbed her hand. "The kids?"

"Books," she suggested, and moved in the direction of the bookstore. She stopped when it became clear Scott wasn't about to follow her.

He frowned and shook his head. "No books."

She realized he hadn't released her hand. "Not cool enough for the new uncle?"

"Precisely."

Evie took a few seconds, then rattled off a couple of other options. Once Scott agreed to one of her suggestions, they headed for the toy store. And the fact that he still held her hand felt ridiculously natural. They walked through the mall and Evie didn't miss how other women blatantly checked him out. A trio of pretty and preened twentysomethings sashayed past and one said something outrageously flirtatious toward Scott. Another from the group looked Evie up and down and raised her brows. At that moment Evie felt about as old as Methuselah. She pulled her hand from his and crossed her arms.

"Something wrong?" Scott asked, seemingly oblivious of the attention he'd garnered as they walked into the toy store.

"Not a thing," she lied, and wished a great big hole would open up and suck her in.

What am I thinking? I'm thirty-six years old... He's twenty-seven. I'm sensible. I should know better than to think this means anything. I don't want it to mean any-

thing...right? It's just sex. Sex without commitment that I said I could handle. No strings. No attachment.

And thinking that, Evie realized, had suddenly become her undoing.

Scott was neck deep in trouble. He'd been determined not to get involved with Evie. And now he felt *so* involved he could hardly think straight. Evie was like...she was like the skin growing over his bones, the air in his lungs. Like no other woman he'd ever met.

Maybe it's just because last night I had the best sex I've had in my life.

Sex could do that, right? Especially incredible, mind-blowing sex. It could warp a man's reality; it could make him think things, *feel* things, wish for things.

But wishes were for fools. He was leaving in two weeks. He knew better than to start something. Two weeks and he couldn't keep his fly zipped. Scott wondered if she'd want to make love again. He wondered how he'd react if she did...or didn't.

As he bought toys for the kids, she kept her distance. Even as they headed for the gift-wrapping booth, she remained quiet. The regret she clearly felt seemed like a force field over her skin. He followed her to the music store and agreed with her suggestion of a gift for Callie's teenage step daughter, Lily. Once the kids were sorted, Scott headed for a jewelry store to purchase something for his mother.

"What about this?" he asked Evie, ignoring the pushy salesclerk who batted her eyelashes at him as he dangled a gold chain from his fingertips.

She shrugged and then nodded. "You know what your mother likes."

"I'm asking if *you* like it."

He got her attention back and she slid sideways, bumping her hip against the counter. "It's pretty."

Scott got a quick image in his head of Evie wearing the necklace around her beautiful neck and nothing else. He shook the thought off and looked briefly at the clerk. "Bracelets."

Minutes later he'd made a selection and the item was wrapped and paid for and they headed from the store. She declined coffee, cake and everything else he suggested. He wasn't sure what he wanted. Being around her messed with his concentration and determination to stay focused on getting through Christmas and the wedding before heading back to L.A. where his job was waiting. The job he was determined he could do without distraction. But *not* being around Evie didn't appeal, either. So he was screwed either way.

There was an uneasy tension between them and he didn't like it one bit.

Scott drove her home and she didn't wait for the keys or for him to haul his shopping bags from the rear seat. Back in his room he could hear her moving around the house, heard the telephone ring, heard the sound of low voices downstairs and imagined her explaining her absence to the ever-curious and relentless Manning sisters. With a brisk shake he decided to stop hiding in his room. He took off immediately and headed downstairs. The sisters passed him in the hallway, all smiles, and made their way out the front door. He waited until they were out of sight and headed for the front living room.

Evie was near the huge Christmas tree, fiddling with ornaments. She still wore her jeans and the tight tank shirt that had been tantalizing him all morning. He'd barely touched her while they were out, only taking her hand once or twice. Casual, that's what he'd thought. But looking at her shapely bottom, he didn't feel at all casual. He was aroused just by the sight of her.

"Callie called," she said, and didn't turn around. He wondered how she'd sensed he was there. "She said to remind you about your mother arriving tomorrow."

"Yeah, I know."

She straightened her shoulders, still fiddling, still with her back to him. "You can put the gifts for the kids under the tree if you like. Unless…unless you're still moving out."

Moving out? That's right. That's what he'd said. That's what he'd decided to do the day before. Move out and away from temptation. And complication. *Too little too late.*

"Is that what you want?"

She shrugged and continued her attention on the already perfect tree. "It's not up to me."

Scott took a step toward her. "Evie?"

"I don't know what I want," she said, and turned. Her green eyes shone brightly. "I'm not completely naive—I know a situation like this is different for a man than it is for a woman. Turns out I'm a whole lot more emotional about having a physical relationship with someone than I thought. We agreed it would be just sex, but I'm not really made that way. So I think it would be better if we went back to how things used to be."

Scott stared at her. *I'm off the hook.* Only, he wasn't so sure he wanted to be.

She turned back to the tree. "I'm going to be in the studio for the next few hours. Please help yourself to anything you want."

Just not me…

Scott got the message. He lingered in the living room for about three seconds before he turned on his heel and left.

Chapter Nine

While she was having her fitting for her bridesmaid dress on Monday afternoon, Evie did her best to appear as much her usual self as possible. Her friend Fiona wasn't fooled, though, and asked her straight-out what was going on with her. Evie shrugged off the question and avoided making eye contact with Callie.

But Fiona didn't give up. "You're distracted."

Evie stood in the dressing cubicle and unzipped the pale gold satin gown and allowed the strapless bodice to hang on one hip. "I'm fine," she replied.

In truth, she was so far from being *fine,* and her head hurt thinking about it.

"You know," Fiona said with a laugh, "that new teacher at school asked about you again."

The third time in as many months. Maybe she should go out with him. At least it might take her mind off Scott. "So set me up."

Her friend's eyes popped wide. "You want a date?"

Evie shrugged. "Don't look so shocked."

"I am shocked," Fiona replied.

"Me, too," Callie said, tapping on the door.

"Well, don't be," Evie said sharply, and pushed at the cubicle doors. "So, can you wrangle it?"

Fiona nodded. "For sure. I just can't believe you're actually going to go on a date with him."

"Why not?"

"Because you don't date," Fiona replied. "Ever."

She experienced a weird dip in her stomach. "Maybe I'm tired of being predictable."

"Ha…not likely. Anyway, he's nice enough. He's a little…"

"A little what?" Callie prompted.

Fiona made a clucking sound. "Dull," she said finally. *Well, what's wrong with being dull? At least he's my own age, lives in the same town and isn't likely to go running into burning buildings any time soon.* "Dull suits me just fine. I like *dull*."

Fiona snorted and Callie laughed and when Evie finally emerged from the dressing cubicle, both her friends were staring at her with lifted brows.

"You don't actually believe that?" Callie asked, and took the dress from Evie's hands.

"Sure I do," she said, and stepped out to allow Fiona inside to try her gown on. "Dull isn't as bad as it sounds. Dull is…" *Safe, reliable, not likely to break my heart.* "Besides, I've met him several times when I've dropped the twins to school and he seemed friendly and pleasant and—"

"Pleasant?" Callie groaned. "Now I know you must be joking."

Evie stood her ground. "Not everyone gets fireworks," she said, holding her ground. "Or wants them."

"What about plain old he-makes-me-weak-at-the-knees lust?" Fiona piped in from behind the door. "That's gotta count."

"Overrated," Evie replied, and tried not to have a flashback about making love with Scott.

"I used to think so," Callie said with a dreamy grin. "I don't think I ever believed in all that romantic stuff before I met Noah—I was always practical and levelheaded when it came to romance. And then I met your brother and *whoosh*…all my practicalities went out the window."

Evie made a face. "Have you been reading Fiona's bodice ripper novels again?"

"You can scorn all you like," Callie said. "But when it happens…watch out."

"I believe in it," Fiona said as she opened the door and stuck out her head and looked directly at Evie. "And however much you deny it, so do you."

"Just ask him, will you?" she said flatly.

Neither woman said anything else.

When she arrived home, Trevor was in the upstairs kitchen making a snack. Evie plonked her bag on the table and took the half ham-and-cheese sandwich he offered. The school term was over, and once the wedding and Christmas were done, her son would be taking his annual trip north to spend a few weeks with Gordon's parents. She always missed him terribly but knew how much her in-laws loved seeing their only grandson. They still invited Evie every year. In the early years after Gordon's death, she'd made the trip several times. But the Dunns' grief was still inconsolable and each year it became harder to face. So she took the coward's way and used the B and B as an excuse to stay behind. She knew they adored having Trevor for those few weeks and wanted her son to have a strong relationship with both sets of grandparents.

"How's the hoop shooting going?" she asked, and took a bite of sandwich.

"Scott reckons I'm a natural," he boasted with a broad grin. "Tryouts are on soon."

"You guys seem to be getting along okay."

Trevor shrugged. "Sure. He's really cool. He knows about computers, too. And mechanics."

The hero worship in her son's voice was glaringly obvious. And she couldn't blame Trevor for feeling like that. Other than her own father and Noah, her son had spent years without having a man's regular influence in his life. "I'm glad you get along."

"Yeah…it's too bad he's leaving soon."

Too bad. Evie couldn't stop her heart tightening up. "Well, Callie lives here now, so the chances are he'll come back to visit his sister."

Even as she said it Evie didn't believe it. Maybe she didn't want to believe it. She'd put the stops on their relationship. She was the one who couldn't do casual. Now the idea of Scott returning to Crystal Point in the future wasn't something she wanted to face. Especially if he didn't come alone. That would be the inevitable future, right? He'd go home, meet someone suitable, eventually fall in love and discard all his protestations about the job and relationships not working for him.

And I'll still be alone.

"I hope so," Trevor said cheerfully.

Evie took a deep breath. "So, how about helping me wrap some gifts?" she suggested, eager to do anything to dislodge the heavy pain inside. "I picked up a few things before my dress fitting today. I could use a hand getting them done."

"Sure," her son said. "But I'm heading to Cody's tonight if that's okay. His dad got him this new computer game for Christmas."

Cody's father was a soldier on tour in Afghanistan. She knew her son's best friend would rather have had his dad home for Christmas than a game for his computer, and was glad her son could be there for his friend.

Evie didn't see Scott that evening. By the time she heard his motorcycle in the driveway, it was well past ten o'clock. She knew he'd been at Callie and Noah's. His mother had arrived from L.A. and it wasn't hard to figure they would want to spend some time together as a family. Evie knew her parents were there, too, which didn't help the tiny stab of exclusion she experienced every time she thought about it.

As it got closer to Christmas Eve she had her routine down. She saw Scott briefly each morning, though they rarely met for breakfast. He spent some time with Trevor and disappeared most days and evenings. So she got exactly what she wanted. They spent a week barely exchanging words, passing each other in the stairway or kitchen. And Evie had also spent the week pulling mistletoe down from around the house. The Manning sisters were clearly the culprits. Evie tossed the stuff in the garbage every time she got her hands on it, much to Flora's and Amelia's amusement.

She had a last-minute panicked phone call from the wedding caterers, but everything else associated with her brother's Christmas Eve wedding went to plan and Evie was convinced that the ceremony would go off without a hitch. Until the day before the wedding. And it wasn't exactly a *hitch*...just a minor catastrophe. One of the groomsmen broke his foot in a boating accident and Callie insisted Scott fill in the role, as well as giving the bride away. Which meant *she* would be partnered with him all evening…at the ceremony, at the reception…and on the dance floor.

The bride and maids were all dressing at Dunn Inn, and the ceremony and reception were being held at the local country club under a huge white silk marquee. Beneath the marquee were hundreds of tiny lights, tables, chairs, a dance floor and a team of smartly attired wait staff.

At the house, Grace was on hand, helping the attendants with hair and makeup. Evie's dress fit like a glove and as Grace fussed with her hair Evie stood compliant and silent. But her sister wasn't fooled.

"Why do you look like you want to be somewhere else?" Grace remarked in a soft voice close to her ear. "Trouble in paradise?"

With Callie on the other side of the room, looking perfectly beautiful in her pale ivory organza gown, Evie knew it wasn't the time for a heart-to-heart with her sister. Fiona and Lily were fiddling with Callie's veil, and Noah's youngest daughter, Hayley, stood by the armoire in the corner twirling on her gold slippers.

There was a short rap on the door, and Grace invited whoever it was to open up. The door swung back and Scott stood beneath the threshold. Evie's skin warmed instantly. He looked incredible in the dark suit, shirt and pale gold tie, and his gaze traveled over her in that way she'd become accustomed to. It had been days since they'd shared such a look, and the silence that overtook the room was suddenly deafening. Everyone noticed. *How could they not?*

Grace said something and Evie quickly scrambled her wits together. "Yes…we're all ready," she said, and ushered Hayley from the corner.

Callie came forward and took his arm. "You look

amazing," Scott said to his sister as he kissed her cheek. "Noah's a lucky man."

Eve's throat tightened. She knew how much Noah and Callie loved each other. She'd watched their relationship blossom barely months ago and couldn't be happier for her brother and soon-to-be bride.

And that thought only made her yearn, suddenly, for happiness of her own.

Watching his sister get married, Scott experienced varying degrees of emotion. As he gave the bride away and stepped aside to stand next to Evie, tightness uncurled in his chest. They were close and he couldn't push away the need to touch her. So he rested the back of his hand against her arm and traced a little path up and down. She shivered but didn't move, didn't do anything that might distract from the bride and groom exchanging their vows.

Once the vows were over, the bridal party disappeared for an hour with the photographer. They were ferried away in golf carts to a spot in the grounds of the country club where they could get the best shots. When they returned to the marquee, most of the guests were already seated.

After dinner there were speeches, the traditional cutting of the cake and then dancing. His sister and new husband took to the floor before the rest of the bridal party followed. To have Evie in his arms felt good.

"I have two left feet," Evie warned, moving to the dance floor with him.

Scott grinned when she began to move in an awkward way. Okay, so Evie couldn't dance. She had other talents. She could cook. And paint. And she was a great kisser.

"You're smiling," she said, and tightened her grip on his shoulder. "Am I that bad?"

"Yep." He chuckled. "Follow my lead and no one will notice. Besides, the bride and groom get all the attention."

She looked across the dance floor to where Noah and Callie swayed together. "Yes, I suppose they do."

He heard a break in her voice. "Evie," he said softly. "Are you all right?"

"I'm fine. Just tired, I guess."

He wondered if she was thinking about her own wedding. That was normal, right? She looked lost and a little sad. She was probably thinking about her husband. The one man she'd loved. The urge to make it better for her drummed through Scott's blood. Not that he knew how. He didn't know much of anything when it came to Evie. The last week had been hell. Living with her but barely speaking, walking into rooms that held the lingering scent of her fragrance, working out ways to avoid being alone with her...the whole damn thing had become exhausting.

The truth was he missed her.

And hadn't a clue what to do about it. Another week and he'd be gone. Back to his life and his job and he could forget all about Evie Dunn. He could forget how she felt in his arms and the taste of her kiss. Every ounce of good sense he possessed warned him away from Evie. But the pull back toward her was intense and impossible to ignore.

They danced for a while longer, not speaking, only moving together. At one point he switched partners with Cameron, the best man, and ended up dancing with a bubbly redhead whose name he didn't quite recall. Later he tried to get Evie alone again. Instead, his sister cornered him by the drinks table.

"Is something going on you're not telling me?" she asked suspiciously.

Scott shrugged and took an imported beer from the bar attendant. "Not a thing."

"You always were a terrible liar."

"Nothing to tell," he assured his sister. "Wanna dance?"

Callie gripped his arm. "I just don't want to see anyone get hurt."

Neither do I. "No one's getting hurt," he said, and took Callie's arm. "Promise."

But as he took his sister to the dance floor, the word felt flat and empty. Because people *were* getting hurt. He was hurting Evie simply by being himself. She'd let him off the hook and he was glad for it...right? He didn't want commitment or anything resembling a relationship.

Only...watching Evie beneath the marquee, shimmering so beautifully in her gold dress, with her magnificent hair curling around her shoulders, it sure as hell felt as though he did.

Because it was Christmas Eve, the wedding was over by nine o'clock. Callie and Noah had planned to spend the next few days at home and were flying out to Hawaii for their honeymoon after New Year's. While they were gone, Mary-Jayne and Callie's mother, Eleanor, would be staying at their place to look after the children.

Evie arrived home at nine-thirty, achingly aware of Scott's presence beside her as he drove her car, and with Trevor in tow, complaining about the penguin suit he'd been forced to wear all afternoon. The Manning sisters were still awake, eager to know all about the wedding, and she remained downstairs for a while to chat with them. Scott and Trevor headed upstairs, presumably to ditch the suits in favor of something less formal. But Evie was reluctant to take off the pale gold satin dress she knew was a flattering fit and color. And the pumps on her feet gave her an extra three inches of height.

The Manning sisters were well into the Christmas cake

and cranberry punch Evie had left out earlier, and she joined them for a glass. When Trevor returned downstairs he swiped some cake and dropped into a chair. It was their usual Christmas Eve tradition—drinks with Flora and Amelia, the retelling of old stories, the exchange of gifts with the sisters and then bed at a respectable hour.

Scott came back downstairs, still in his suit minus the tie, and Evie's pulse jumped about erratically. She wondered how she'd ever find any man attractive again after he disappeared from her life. He held a carry bag and she recognized the name of the gift store in Bellandale. The sisters were delighted he had joined them and they all found a spot in the living room around the big tree and began exchanging gifts.

Trevor was blown away by the newest computer game Scott gave him, and the sisters appreciated the trinkets he gifted them with. Evie was touched, imagining him selecting presents for the elderly women. She didn't say much as she accepted a beautiful linen tablecloth from the sisters and watched as each opened the set of small watercolors she'd painted years earlier of various scenes from Crystal Point.

"This is for you."

Evie looked up. Scott held out a small parcel and she took it with tentative fingers. Instead of ripping open the wrapping as she was tempted to do, she passed him the gift she'd bought him, but had wondered if she'd have the courage to give him. It was nothing particularly personal— a traveler's guide to historical facts of the local area, but he seemed to like it. Once everyone had finished unwrapping she felt all four sets of eyes focused on her. The gift in her hands remained unopened.

"Oh, of course." She pried open the paper and then lifted the lid on the small box. On a cushion of blue velvet lay a ball of crystal, with an image of a woman cleverly engraved within. "How…lovely."

"It's Catherine of Bologna," he explained. "Patron Saint of Artists."

Evie's heart flipped over. "Thank you." She popped the lid back and stood. "Trevor—time for bed." She looked toward the Manning sisters and not once in Scott's direction. "Well, good night. I'll see you in the morning. Breakfast will be at nine."

She walked from the room with a stiff back, clutching the gift against her ribs. *Any moment now,* she thought… *any second and I will burst into tears.* She got to the kitchen in record time and didn't relax until she heard the familiar thud of feet heading upstairs and the sound of doors closing at the front of the house.

Now I can breathe.

She snuck another look at the crystal globe and shut the box just as quickly. It was too much. That he should know her like this and enter her world with a gift so personal to her, a gift she somehow knew he'd chosen because it *was* personal. No one did that for Evie. No one saw deep inside her or thought to wonder what she needed. Her family and friends gave her crockery and linen and CDs. People who'd known her forever but didn't really know her at all. Didn't know how much pain she felt because her creativity had been zapped. Didn't know how much she longed to be able to put all of her heart into her painting again and feel the passion in each brushstroke.

"You look really beautiful in that dress."

She swiveled around. Scott stood in the doorway.

"I should have said so earlier."

Evie clutched the gift and shrugged a little. "It's okay. Everyone looks at the bride."

He leaned against the doorjamb. "I was looking at you."

Her feelings for him lurched forward, catching her breath with an unexpected intensity. "I thought you might have spent the evening at your sister's. Your mother's there and Callie would—"

"I wanted to be here," he said quietly, cutting her off. "I'll see my mom and Callie tomorrow."

Evie swallowed hard. "Well, I'm glad you're here. And I know Trevor appreciated it. He doesn't get a lot of adult male company. Well, except for Noah and my father."

And he misses his dad... But Evie didn't say it, she didn't imply that her son was longing for another father figure in his life. Or that she wanted Scott to fill the role. She wasn't about to start wishing for what could never be.

"You look really beautiful in that dress."

She placed the gift on the bench top. "You said that already. Thank you for my gift."

He smiled. "I thought she might watch over you while you paint. You know, to help with your muse."

"I hope it will," she replied. "I want to get back into it. I want to find myself in it again."

He hadn't moved. She looked up and spotted a piece of mistletoe hanging above his head, and it made her smile. "Looks like Flora and Amelia have been at it again."

He looked upward. "I guess we shouldn't disappoint them."

She didn't budge. He still hadn't moved, still remained in the doorway, arms crossed, shoulder against the architrave, looking as if he knew she wanted him.

And she did. So much her whole body hurt.

"What if I can't let you go?" she asked shakily.

"You will," he replied. "You're a strong woman. Stronger than you think."

"I'm a fraud," she admitted, taking a step toward him.

"I'm not really the sensible sister. In fact, right now I don't feel the least bit sensible."

"Because you know the odds of a long-distance relationship working out are virtually zero?"

Yes...that's why. And because she wanted it to work, the idea shocked her. Lust and desire had morphed into something deeper—something so deep she knew she was in danger of having her heart broken into inconsolable pieces. She tried to marshal her thoughts and feelings and tame the wildness within her blood. But she failed.

"Because I said I couldn't do casual," she said, and took another step. "And because I know that when this is over, I will have to let you go."

He reached for her in three strides and hauled her into his arms, not roughly, but with enough force that Evie sucked in a startled breath as his mouth found hers. His kiss was hot and hard, his tongue a driving force against the softness of her lips. And she craved it. She craved it and took everything, every slide, every slant, every part of him he was willing to give her. She was hot all over, like a raging furnace, and she'd never been more alive in her life.

His hands gripped her shoulders, molding her against him, and still he kissed her. Evie pushed herself against him, wanting to feel as close as she could with clothes on. He groaned low in his throat and deepened the kiss, drawing her into his mouth.

Scott's hands roamed down her body and settled on her bottom. "Did I tell you how beautiful you look in that dress?" he asked against her mouth, and ground their hips together.

Evie smiled. "You may have mentioned it."

"But right now," he growled, "I just wanna get you out of it."

It took about two minutes to get to Scott's room and

about thirty seconds to remove their clothes. They made love quickly, passionately and without words. Evie clung to him, taking and giving, feeling him all over her, around her and finally inside her. She gave herself up to the pleasure and came apart in his arms. When he lost himself, too, she clung to him tightly, watching in amazement as his strong body shuddered and then lay still against her.

She touched his back, trailing her fingers up and down his spine. He was breathing heavy and took a few gulps of air before he rolled from her and flung himself onto his back.

In the darkness, with only the sound of the waves crashing against the rocks along the foreshore intruding on them, Evie let out a long sigh of contentment. She felt a lovely sense of lethargy. She touched his arm and was startled to feel the tenseness in his muscles.

"Evie?"

She held her breath for a second. Did he regret their lovemaking? "Yes?"

"I didn't protect you." His words echoed around the room. "I'm sorry."

They hadn't used a condom. She quickly did a math calculation in her head. "It's fine," she assured him, but tiny fingers of concern clutched at her veins. She stroked his arm. "No need to worry."

"I don't have unprotected sex, ever."

She twisted her lips. "Except for just now."

"Well...yeah. Is there any chance you might get—"

"No," she said quickly. "No, I don't think...no," she said again. "Very little chance."

Very little chance? Just what did that mean? Scott couldn't believe his carelessness. He never played roulette with birth control. He sat up in bed and flicked on the light. "You're sure?"

Evie rolled onto her side and raised both brows. "I know my cycle."

His stomach turned over. She looked so calm and it annoyed the hell out of him. "You'd tell me?" he asked, almost holding his breath. "If something happened?"

"Well, it's not the sort of thing I could keep a secret, is it?"

She had a point. And the knee-jerk terror he'd felt gradually dissipated. He reached into the bedside drawer and grabbed a foil packet. "No more roulette," he said, and tossed it onto the bed. "For next time."

"Next time?" Evie picked up the protection and held it between two fingers. "You're that sure there'll be a next time?"

Scott smiled, rolled over and pinned her beneath him. "I'm sure," he said, trailing kisses along her collarbone, "that I won't get through the next hour unless I can make love to you again."

Evie kissed his jaw. "So stop talking and get to it."

Shortly afterward they made love again, this time with protection, and then they took a shower together.

"I have a spa bath in my ensuite bathroom," she told him as she blotted her skin dry with a towel. "That could be fun."

"Is that an invitation to enter the inner sanctum of your bedroom?"

She stopped toweling. "What does that mean?"

Scott wrapped a towel around his waist. "You know exactly what it means."

She draped the towel around herself toga-style. "You think I'm keeping my bedroom off-limits?" She frowned. "And why would I want to do that?"

Suddenly, the steam in the room was coming off Evie and not from the hot water. "You tell me?"

"You know," she said, twisting her hair free from the towel she had wrapped around it to keep it dry, "that's a pretty adolescent answer."

Scott felt the bite of her remark. "Are you denying it?"

"I'm saying I haven't consciously acted that way."

Scott didn't push the issue, but he certainly felt her reluctance to share her room with him. "Okay. Let's forget it."

Evie tucked at her towel. "I should probably go to my room anyway," she said quietly as she walked from the bathroom and into the bedroom. "Trevor normally comes to see me first thing—you know, it being Christmas in about an hour."

"Sure," he said with about as much enthusiasm as a rock.

He stayed by the door and watched as she collected the dress he'd stripped off her earlier. She grabbed her shoes and underwear and headed for the door. She turned before she grabbed the handle. "Well, good night."

Scott remained where he was and pushed back the fierce pounding inside his chest and the urge to ask her to stay, and the need to take back his stupid comment about her bedroom. He'd never been the jealous type—maybe because he'd never cared enough to feel the gut-wrenching emotion before this…before Evie. But he was jealous. He was jealous she'd kept that part of her from him…from *them*.

At that moment, as if he'd been hit with a thunderbolt, Scott realized just how powerful his feelings for Evie had become.

"When this is over I will have to let you go."

He knew that. She wouldn't make a scene. She'd don her Sensible Evie hat and send him on his way, back to his life in L.A., back to everything and everyone who was familiar to him—and not one of them, he knew, could hold a candle to the woman in front of him.

"Good night, Evie," he said. "Merry Christmas."

She left the room without another word.

Chapter Ten

Christmas at Barbara and Bill Preston's house was a day-long celebration that started in the morning and only finished when Evie's dad fell asleep in his favorite recliner and the kids started dozing off because they'd consumed copious amounts of pop and candy. But it had been a good day. With her entire family in attendance, plus the whole Jakowski clan, the Manning sisters and a few other people long regarded as family, it was a day to remember.

Of course, Evie hardly spoke to Scott. She made sure she was well away from him at the long table when dinner was served, and avoided eye contact as much as possible. No one could know they were lovers. No one could know she craved him in ways she hadn't imagined possible. There was no point. He'd be gone in a week and she'd go back to the structured and predictable life she'd had before he'd entered her world. And she fooled everyone.

Except Grace.

Her smart, mostly aloof sister was onto her.

"You've been to L.A., haven't you?" Grace asked quietly. She'd sidled up to Evie as she scraped plates of uneaten food into a plastic bag. "I went to a conference there a few years back. Good weather, friendly people. Quite a lot like here, actually. You'd probably like to go back and revisit the sights, right?"

Evie continued her task and didn't flinch. "Is there a point to this conversation?"

Grace raised her perfect brows. "Of course. You'd need someone to show you around. Quite the coincidence that Scott is—"

"Would you stop," Evie demanded. "We're not—"

"Oh, spare me," Grace said, cutting her off. "Despite how hard you've tried not to show it, if you two were any more into each other I'd have to get the hose out."

Evie's face burned. "I can't believe you just said that." She tied the plastic bag in a tight knot. "It's impossible, anyhow."

Grace moved alongside her. "So you're involved?"

"We're something… I'm not sure what."

"Lovers?" Grace asked.

Evie's cheeks flamed. "It's new for me. I've never had a lover before. I mean, other than Gordon. But Scott makes me feel so…so…" She shrugged. *"Whoosh."*

Grace's faultlessly beautiful face creased in a frown. "What?"

"You know," Evie explained. "That thing…that feeling. Not that I'm an expert, but Fiona and Callie assured me it's called *whoosh*."

Her sister looked mildly amused. "So what are you going to do about it?"

"Do? Nothing. Just get back to my real life when it's over."

"Perhaps this is your real life," Grace said.

Evie gave her younger sister a startled stare. No, she thought. Her real life was the B and B and being a mother and a friend and a sister and a daughter. Being Scott's lover was only ever going to be temporary. She raised her hands and twirled them in the air. "This is my real life."

Grace smiled and exposed perfectly white teeth. "Don't sell yourself short."

She found it a strange comment from her usually tight-lipped sister—it was Mary-Jayne who always dispensed advice on romance. "I won't."

"Not that I'm an expert in the area," Grace said. "In fact, forget I said anything. Perhaps I'm feeling more optimistic than usual at the moment."

"Really?" she asked, knowing there was something going on with her sister. At another time she would have asked. She would have donned her *sympathetic* cap and listened with an open mind and heart. But not today. Her heart was full. Her mind was muddled.

And later that night as she lay snuggled up to Scott after making love with him, Evie experienced the profound realization that she wanted to stay in his arms for the rest of her life.

Scott was certain the days got shorter the closer he came to leaving Crystal Point and returning to Los Angeles.

"I like your mother," Evie said to him one night, curled up against him after they'd made love. "We got to talk a bit today. She's nice."

"Did you?" He trailed his fingers along her shoulder. "Do you think she's worked it out? Us, I mean?"

Evie shrugged. "I'm not sure. Would she mind?"

"About you?" He smiled. "Hardly. She's happy if I'm happy."

Evie's inside jumped. It sounded so incredibly inti-mate. Scott was happy with her? She didn't dare imagine what that meant. "And she never remarried after your dad passed away?"

"Nope."

"She must have loved him deeply. I mean to never have another man in her life."

"She did," he replied, and suddenly he was thinking about Evie and not his mother. Evie hadn't remarried. Evie had stayed true to her husband. Except for now, he thought, feeling the smoothness of her lovely skin against him. Feel-ing Evie all over him, inside, as if she were the air in his lungs. How would he ever breathe again once he left her?

"How did they meet?"

Scott shuffled his thoughts to her question. "They met when they were twenty. My dad and his twin sister moved to L.A. when they were twenty and got jobs working with a telecommunications company. They were only meant to be gone twelve months. Turns out they stayed for good."

Eve cuddled closer. "Was he sick for a long time?"

Scott's chest tightened. "Yes. He'd been in a bad acci-dent a few years before and afterward was plagued by the side effects and related illnesses."

"What kind of accident?"

"He was a climber," he said, thinking that would be enough. "A mountaineer."

Evie shifted on her side and looked at him. "Tell me about his accident."

Scott closed his eyes for a moment, remembering what had happened as though it were yesterday. "He was on an expedition to Nanga Parbat, the second highest peak in Pakistan. He suffered from high-altitude edema and almost lost his life. Fortunately his team got him down in time. He came home to us and died a couple of years later. He didn't have the lungs to climb again. Sometimes I think that *not* climbing was more responsible for his death than the peak itself."

"I didn't realize he was an—"

"Adrenaline junkie?" He cut her off gently. "Yes, he was."

"Did you ever climb with him?"

"I did not." It came out harsher than he liked, but a swell of feelings washed up in his chest, mixing with the sudden desire *not* to talk about his father.

Evie picked up on it immediately. "You didn't approve?"

Scott shrugged. "It wasn't my place to approve. It was his life."

"A life he risked?"

Scott felt the truth burn through his blood. And the lingering resentment for a man who was essentially a good father—although sometimes a reckless one. "Like I said, it was his—"

"You don't believe that," she said, cutting him off as she sat up. "I don't get it—you obviously have a problem with what your dad did and yet you chose to become a firefighter."

"One has nothing to do with the other."

Evie made a huffing sound. "Yeah—right. One is *all* about the other."

"My father climbed mountains for the thrill of the climb—I do not fight fires for that reason." He pushed at the bedclothes and sat up. "It's a job, Evie."

She scooted across the bed until she was in front of him. The light of the half-moon shone through the open curtains and when the sheet she'd been trying to hold slipped away, Scott got a great look at her rose-tipped breasts. His body stirred instantly and he grazed the back of his hand over one nipple.

"Stop doing that," she said, probably not as sharp as she wanted as she pulled back. "I want to talk with you. Don't distract me."

Scott's eyes widened. "You're distracting me," he assured her as he looked at her breasts.

Evie unexpectedly reached out and touched his face, lifting his cheek upward so their eyes met. "Tell me why you really became a firefighter."

Scott took a breath. "Because I wanted to run into burning buildings."

"And that's all?"

"Isn't that enough?" he asked. "It's what you believe, anyway—isn't it?'

"I'm not so sure anymore."

"Believe it," he said, but the truth suddenly jumped around in his head. He reached for her, dragging her against him as he pushed back against the pillows. Enough talk, he thought. Enough truth. He took her mouth in a searing kiss that was so hot it practically scorched the air between them. Her mouth was sweet and tempting and luscious. He'd kiss her and forget the days were closing in. He'd make love with her and disregard the taunting voice in the back of his mind reminding him that the heaven he'd found in Evie's arms was only ever going to be temporary. She *would* let him go. And he would have to leave and return to reality.

Evie got home to an empty house on the Tuesday after Christmas. When she reached the upstairs kitchen she found a note stuck near the telephone written in her son's neat handwriting. *Have gone out with Scott—be back later.*

Evie's heart stilled. Trevor was with Scott. And Scott, she knew, was at the Emergency Services Station, speaking with the volunteers and the local Rural Fire Brigade.

Anger quickly filled her blood and she grabbed her car keys.

He wouldn't do that. Surely he'd know I'd never agree to that.

The drive took only a few minutes. Evie parked outside and jumped out of the car. She saw Scott's motorcycle and the vehicles of the other volunteers. Her blood pumped, her thoughts suddenly centered on Trevor being here, with these people. *These people I've considered the enemy for ten years.* Maybe not consciously, but in her secret place, her darkest heart.

She reached the doorway and stood beneath the threshold. The big shed was filled with people and she felt the gut-wrenching pain she always felt when confronted with this place. She always stayed outside, never going into the big, cold building with its corrugated walls and concrete floor. Memories bombarded Evie's thoughts. Memories of Gordon's lifeless body lying on the floor—and thoughts of well-meaning colleagues hovering around him, trying to revive him, trying to bring him back.

By the time Evie had arrived, he'd gone. There were no goodbyes. Just his battered body left stretched out on the cold floor, covered in a plastic tarp so she wouldn't see the extent of his injuries.

She hated this place.

There was a group of people behind the fire truck, positioned in a half arc. Scott stood in the center beside a long white board and was talking to the Rural Fire Brigade volunteers in a quiet voice. She loved his voice, loved hearing him whisper things to her as they made love. Loved hearing him say she was beautiful, desirable…loved the soft pleas of encouragement against her skin when she touched him a certain way or in a certain place.

But he wasn't speaking those words now. Now he was

all-business, pure firefighter and every inch the man who risked his life daily because that was his job. Evie watched for a moment, half absorbed, half repulsed. Until she spotted Trevor. Her son was listening intently and wearing a yellow jacket, the same type of high-visibility gear the volunteers wore.

She saw red immediately. "Trevor?" About a dozen sets of eyes zoomed in on her, including her son's. But it was Scott's gaze she felt snap through her with blistering intensity. He stared at her, frowning, and she turned immediately back to her son. "Let's go home."

The silence continued. Everyone there knew her of course—she was poor Evie Dunn who'd lost her husband. They offered pity in their stares and it made her so mad she wanted to shout and tell them they were all reckless fools.

"But I was just—"

Evie raised her hand and beckoned him forward. "Come on," she said, before she swiveled on her heels and headed back to the car with Trevor in tow. He was complaining, but Evie was in no mood to listen. She told him to take off the jacket and he handed it to her after a few seconds of resistance.

"Evie, wait up."

She stilled instantly, told Trevor to get into the car and then turned and took the dozen or so steps to reach Scott. "How could you do it?" she demanded, her voice higher than she wanted, her heart pounding the blood through her veins.

"How could I do what?"

Evie glared at him, so angry she could barely get the words out. "How could you bring my son here?"

He looked at her oddly. "I don't—"

"You had no right," she said, and pushed away the hotness behind her eyes. "I don't want him here with these people."

"What people?"

Evie pointed toward the building. "The people who knew his father. People who did what Gordon did. People who were with him *that night*."

"Evie," he said quietly, "I had no intention of—"

"Don't you get it?" she snapped, and tossed the jacket into his chest. He caught it immediately. "I don't want him here." She waved her arms. "He can't want this like his father did. I don't want him to be like Gordon. And I certainly don't want him to be like you."

The pain in Evie's voice cut through Scott. *"I don't want him to be like you."* He wasn't sure what to think. He heard her anguish and fought the instinctive urge to take her in his arms.

"Evie, I'm sorry if I've upset you. I didn't realize you'd have a problem with Trevor coming with me."

She made a huffing sound. "You should have asked permission. He's *my* son."

"He asked to come with me," Scott explained. "I didn't drag him here."

"He's a child. My child!" She crossed her arms jerkily, her anger palpable. "And I decide where he goes and who he goes with."

"Okay," he said, feeling less than agreeable but refusing to trade any more heated words with her while they were out in the open and at risk of being overheard, not only by Trevor but also by the dozen volunteers inside the shed. "We can talk about this later."

She seemed to calm for a moment, and took a step forward. But she wasn't calm at all, he noticed; she was furious—and all her fury was absolutely aimed toward him.

"Don't try to pacify me, Scott." She planted her hands firmly on her hips. "You can play superhero with these people all you like—but don't ever involve my son."

"Superhero?" he echoed incredulously. "What does that mean?"

"You know exactly. I saw you in there. You were holding court with the volunteers, and they were listening to you like you're some kind of fire god. Well, maybe to them you are. But not to me." She tossed her hair. "To me you're just…just…you're…"

Scott wasn't sure he wanted to hear. "I'm what?"

She glared at him and whispered, "A mistake." With a spin, she turned away and stomped toward her small car. Scott watched wordlessly as she flung herself inside and drove off.

He remained where he was, feeling her words like a fist to his gut. After a moment, he turned around to find Cameron Jakowski standing a few feet away. He shrugged.

"If it makes you feel better," Cameron said quietly, "it's more about what happened here than you letting Trev tag along. Gordon was brought here the night he died."

Scott's stomach rolled. He pointed to the building. "Here?"

Cameron nodded. "Yeah. It was a pretty bad scene that night. There was no chance of the paramedics getting to him in time—his injuries were too extensive. He was crushed between two trailers at the holiday park. They brought him here and this is where he died."

Scott felt a burning pressure gather behind his ribs. He left about an hour later determined to straighten the mess out with Evie.

It was well past six o'clock when he returned to Dunn Inn. The big house seemed eerily quiet. The lights from the Christmas tree blinked through the front window, and he headed for the room when he spotted Evie's unmistakable silhouette moving back and forth through the curtains.

"Can we talk?"

She was by the sofa, fluffing cushions, and didn't stop her task as she spoke. "I'd rather not."

Scott took a few steps into the room. "Well, how about I talk and you listen?"

That got her attention and she stopped what she was doing. "Okay...talk."

Scott pushed down the annoyance in his throat. "I'm sorry."

"Fine," she said tersely, and continued moving pillows. "You're sorry."

"Cameron told me about your husband."

She looked across the room. "He did? And what did he say? That Gordon's body was left at that place for seven hours? That I wasn't allowed to see him because his injuries were so bad? That his blood-soaked jacket was lying on the floor for everyone to see? The same kind of jacket Trevor was wearing tonight. Or that I had to tell my five-year-old son his daddy wouldn't be coming home?"

Scott chose his words carefully. "It must have been a difficult time."

"It was the worst moment of my life."

"And seeing Trevor there brought it all back?"

"Yes. And I don't want my son involved in that life."

Scott took a few steps toward her. "But if that's what he chooses, Evie, all you can really do is support him."

"Are you a parenting expert now?"

It was such an unlike-Evie thing to say that Scott felt the sting of it through to his bones. "No—but I know you can't make someone be something they're not."

Evie raised her chin. "My son is going to college, and

then he'll choose whatever career suits him. He won't be risking his life pursing pointless adventure."

A kernel of resentment sprouted inside him. She was so wrong. "I hardly think that an Emergency Services volunteer is looking for pointless adventure—it takes a certain kind of selflessness to risk one's own life to ensure the safety of someone else."

"Well, you would think that," she said, not looking the least bit convinced. "But I know most of those people that were there this afternoon. They were Gordon's friends— they're the same people he used to bungee jump with and deep-sea-dive with and when they had a chance would climb every rock face they could find. They have the same rogue gene he had—that need to push to the limit, to try something purely because it was dangerous." She sat down on the sofa. "That's not a legacy I want my son to inherit."

So her husband had an adventurous spirit. It began to make sense to him now. "It was a bad storm that killed your husband, Evie, not extreme sports."

"It was the thrill," she said coolly. "The thrill of beating human mortality. Wasn't your own father one of them? I should think you'd understand my determination to keep Trevor away from those people."

"I do understand. But I also know that the volunteers I was with this afternoon are good people who care for their community and want to give something back. They're not thrill seekers, Evie."

"*I* know them," she said quietly. "I know what makes them tick. I know that on the night of the cyclone, Gordon couldn't wait to get out there—he couldn't wait to put on his jacket and face the elements. Because he had no fear and no concern for the consequences. He wanted to fix everything, and in the end he couldn't do the one thing he should have done…kept himself safe…kept himself part of our family. He broke our family apart because he had this need to protect everyone around him."

Realization landed squarely on Scott's shoulders. "Is that why you're so angry? Because he left you that night? Are you mad at him because he went out when he should have stayed home to protect you?"

"No," she said quickly. "Yes. I don't know."

She wrapped her arms around herself and seemed so incredibly vulnerable Scott had to fight his urge to hold her. "I imagine the last thing he expected was that he wouldn't come home to you."

She looked up and met his gaze head-on. "You think I'm being irrational?"

"I think you're…hurting…and maybe a bit misguided."

His words clearly struck a chord because her eyes shone with tears. "I knew you'd never really understand how I feel about this stuff."

"I do understand, Evie."

"How could you? You're a firefighter. Your whole life is a risk. You said yourself that you'd have to quit if you wanted…if you ever wanted something else…more than just the job."

The idea of having more than just the job suddenly seemed very real. And quitting? Scott felt the weight of his words stomp between his shoulder blades. "I know what I said. I watched my friend die because he wanted both…and I watched my father give up time with his family because he was obsessed with his mountains. But the people you think are going to corrupt your son into wanting to risk his life—they're just out to do their bit for their community. I don't think they have lofty ideals about adventure or pushing themselves to the limits for the thrill of it. You're wrong about them, Evie. And you're wrong to not allow your son to get to know his father's friends."

She took a deep breath and glared at him through her tears. "I'm wrong because I want to keep my son safe?"

"You're wrong because you assume everyone's motivation is the same." Scott rested his hands on the back of the sofa. "Do you want to know why I joined the fire department, Evie? Not so I could fulfill some desire for adventure or because I wanted to put my life on the line to satisfy an egotistical need to prove I'm immortal—I joined because I wanted a profession my father would be proud of."

The words seemed truer now than they ever had before, and Scott forced back the lump of emotion suddenly clogging his throat. "He worked behind a desk his whole life, and a couple of times a year he'd take off for his mountains. And each time I'd wonder if this was the last time I'd see him. He wanted me to go with him, he wanted to share it with me, but I was just a scared kid who spent most of my time with my head in a book or playing football. I never went with him. I never got to understand what drew him to risk his life every time he climbed. By the time I'd gotten past my boyhood fears and thought that maybe I *could* go with him, he was dead. So I joined the LAFD and I thought in some way, from wherever he was, he might know I wasn't afraid anymore."

Evie felt the hot sting of tears behind her eyes again and blinked a couple of times. She had a hard time imagining this strong, confident man being afraid of anything. Her feelings for him...her love for him suddenly felt like a powerful, overwhelming force—more intense than anything she had ever known.

But loving him wasn't enough. She'd had a life before Scott entered her world—a life she had to get back to. Sensible Evie was about to make a comeback. She couldn't change who she was—at least not forever. Perhaps for a few stolen weeks. But afterward she would be left with only memories and the knowledge that they were as incompatible as oil and water.

"I need to stay angry with you to help me get through these next few days. I can't sleep with you anymore. I just can't. Good night, Scott," she said quietly, wanting nothing more than to fold herself in his arms and stay there for the rest of her life.

He touched her arm as she walked by him. "Evie," he said, taking her hand. "Is this really how you want it to be?"

"Yes," she said, but wasn't sure how. "I think we both know it's for the best."

His expression was unreadable and he released her instantly. "For the record, Evie, I'll *never* consider what's happened between us a mistake."

Chapter Eleven

Evie stayed downstairs for a while, thinking about Scott, thinking about Trevor. Her son deserved an explanation, so she headed directly for Trevor's room when she got upstairs. He was sitting on the edge of his bed, a handheld computer game at his fingertips.

"Can I come in?"

He shrugged. "Sure."

Evie took a couple of steps into the room. "I'm not mad at you or anything," she said quietly.

He looked up. "You're mad at Scott, though."

She didn't disagree. "He should have asked me if it was okay for you to go with him."

"He didn't force me to go. I tagged along," Trevor said. "I didn't think it would be such a big deal."

A big deal? Evie suddenly felt like an overprotective, cloistering parent who wasn't prepared to give her child the freedom to spread his wings. "I'm sorry if I embarrassed you. It's just that I—"

"Don't want me to end up like Dad," he said, and tossed the game onto the bed. "Yeah, I know."

Shame crept along her spine. "That's not exactly it," she said. "I just want you to have other opportunities."

"I wasn't joining up," he told her. "I wouldn't do that without talking to you about it first. I was just listening. Cody's thinking of volunteering and I thought I'd go along and see what goes on there. But Scott told us we should think about finishing school first because that's our priority at the moment." He raised his brows. "It made sense. So, like I said, I wasn't joining up—I was listening."

Evie wanted to hug him close. Instead she took a deep breath. "I should have trusted you. But when I saw you wearing that jacket I—"

"I was only trying it on. Scott told me to wear it so I could feel how hot it gets inside one of those things. Then he told me to imagine wearing that and a heavy hat and oxygen and then walking into a fire." Trevor held up one skinny arm. "He said he reckoned I needed to do a whole lot of push-ups before I could carry all that equipment."

Evie tried to shake the powerful pounding of her heart. "He's right."

Trevor made a face. "I know he is. You shouldn't be mad at him. I wish he was hanging around."

But he's not.

Three days later Evie said goodbye to Scott. Callie was taking him to the airport and Evie barely registered his quiet farewell. She didn't touch him, didn't kiss him, didn't hang on to him and tell him how much she would miss him, even though the need to do so pumped through her blood with a molten fury. She stood back as he shook Trevor's hand and said goodbye to Flora and Amelia. She didn't look at Callie as he collected his bags and left, terrified her friend would see the truth in her eyes.

Once he'd left she headed directly for her studio. She had managed about ten minutes alone when Flora Manning tapped on the door and didn't wait to be invited inside.

"I'm sorry to see that young man leave," Flora said pointedly.

"His life is in L.A.," Evie said as she grabbed a couple of pots filled with brushes.

Flora raised her silver brows. "Is it?"

Evie dropped the pots into the sink. "I really don't want to—"

"I'm not fooled, you know," she said, cutting her off. "If you had any sense you'd jump into that car of yours and chase after him."

Evie's cheeks flamed. "I *do* have sense," she said quickly. "That's why I'm staying exactly where I am."

"You're stubborn," Flora said. "That's your trouble."

"It's better this way. He can get on with his life…and so can I."

Flora looked around the room. "This isn't your life— this is the place where you hide from life." She tutted. "But enough said. Amelia and I are leaving tomorrow."

And the house would be even quieter. With no new guests arriving for a few weeks, Evie had plenty of time to think about Scott. Plenty of time to remember everything they'd shared. But right now she had to pull herself together and not give in to the dreadful pain in her heart.

"I've enjoyed having you here," Evie said. "And thank you for…well, you know." She reached out and hugged the elderly woman.

"So stop being a damned fool and take what's in front of you," Flora said into her ear.

He's not mine to take...

And knowing that hurt her so much she could barely breathe.

The end of January and all of February were unusually quiet for the B and B. But having only one guest gave Evie an opportunity to get stuck into some necessary cleaning and repair work. She hired a handyman to replace window hinges that had corroded from the salt in the air, a requirement when the ocean was at the doorstep, and set about to do some of the minor painting and yard work by herself.

She went on a date with the schoolteacher, experienced not a single bit of *whoosh* and decided to forget about dating for the next couple of decades.

Summer had arrived with a vengeance. The days were hot, the nights long and balmy. Trevor had gone north to visit Gordon's parents, and without him the big house seemed empty.

To make things worse she caught some kind of bug and was laid up in bed for a few days. Afterward, once the nausea abated, she still couldn't kick the fatigue, and her plans to spend long afternoons in the garden, pruning hedges and repotting geraniums around the wishing well, took a backseat to her sudden need to take a nap almost every afternoon.

And then three weeks after he'd returned to Los Angeles, Evie got an email from Scott. It wasn't particularly personal, just a few short lines asking how she was, and he mentioned that he'd returned to work. After dwelling on it for two days, she wrote back.

January 23
Pleased that you've settled back into your routine. It's

quiet around here at the moment, without any guests and Trevor's away. Take care, Evie.

Twenty-four hours later he sent one back.

January 24
Trev emailed me a few days ago and said he was heading off to his grandparents'. He also said you'd been sick. Are you okay now? Scott.

Evie hadn't realized her son was communicating with Scott. But she wasn't surprised. Trevor was addicted to his computer and had genuinely liked Scott. And Evie had to admit, Scott had been generous with his time in regard to her son. She wrote back a few hours later.

January 24
I'm fine, just the summer flu. Lucky you left when you did or you might have caught my germs. Evie.

January 25
I could think of worse things.

It continued like that for a week. Emails about nothing in particular. Nothing important. He asked how she was doing; she said she was fine. She inquired about his work; he said it was okay. But beneath the surface, something simmered…a kind of tension filled with words unsaid. Finally, on the seventh day, he sent her a message she obsessed over for three days.

February 1
I've been thinking, Evie…and I regret the way things ended between us. I'd like to think we can be friends. Scott.

Friends? Evie wasn't so sure she had the fortitude it would take to remain friends with a man she'd known only as her lover. A man she had fallen in love with and whom she could never have. Between the years that divided them and the career he'd chosen, their differences seemed impossible to overcome now that an ocean lay between them. But he was Callie's brother. He was family. And family was important.

So she garnered her resolve and replied.

February 4
I agree. And I've been thinking too. I overreacted that afternoon. And I'm sorry we didn't really get to say goodbye. Evie.

February 5
Me too. But I'm not sure I could have managed to say goodbye to you.

After that, the emails they exchanged became friendlier and she found herself sharing stories about what was happening in Crystal Point, about her guests who had just arrived and the slow progress being made renovating the surf club. In turn, he told her about his close circle of friends and how the football team he supported was doing and what he'd been creating in the kitchen. He asked if she'd been painting and she admitted that she had been spending time in the studio.

She slept a lot, sometimes in the guest room where she'd spent her magical moments with Scott. She lay on the bed and hugged a pillow, imagining the sheets still had the scent of him in them. But she didn't cry—despite feeling so emotional and wrung out. By the end of February the nausea returned and she began to wonder if something was seriously wrong. Trevor noticed it, too.

"You're sick again?" he asked one afternoon when he loped through the door after school.

Evie shrugged and sat down wearily. "I'm just tired."

Trevor grabbed an apple from the fruit bowl and placed it in front of her. "And you're hardly eating."

That wasn't exactly true. She did eat. Dry toast and crackers seemed to have become her staple diet to combat the wretched nausea. And she was so tired that eating huge meals seemed like way too much effort.

She grabbed the apple and smiled. "I eat," she said, and to prove her point took a tiny bite. "See."

"You've been like this for a month or so. Maybe you should see a doctor?"

Evie looked at her son. A month? Had it been that long? But what would a doctor tell her—to drink fluids and rest? Wasn't that the usual remedy for the flu?

Only, the more she considered it, the less like a flu it seemed. Besides the nausea and fatigue, she didn't feel sick. She felt…like…like…

Evie dropped the apple and quickly excused herself. She headed for her bedroom and grabbed the desk diary in her bedside drawer. She looked at the calendar pages with urgent fingers. The empty pages stared back at her.

I missed my period.

Not once, but twice. *How did I not notice that?*

Oh…God…could it be true? *Could I be pregnant with Scott's baby?* She did the calculation in her head and worked out the weeks. She remembered the time they'd made love without protection. She dropped the diary and placed her hands on her abdomen. A baby? Tears pitched behind her eyes and she shook herself. There was no point in imagining what a baby would mean to her before she had proof.

She took about ten minutes to change her clothes and

grab the keys to her Honda. The trip into town was forty-five minutes there and back, with a quick stop at a pharmacy to purchase an over-the-counter pregnancy test.

She took the test and waited. Three of the longest minutes of her life. Once the time was up, Evie stared at the strip. Two blue lines. She sat on the edge of the bathtub.

Oh, sweet heaven...

"I'm pregnant." She said it out loud. "Oh, my God, I'm pregnant."

I'm having Scott's baby...

Joy and fear mixed together and created a vortex of feelings inside her so intense she stood no chance of stopping the tears. So Evie let them come. When it was over she felt better, stronger somehow, to deal with the inevitable fallout when news of her pregnancy came out. Because it *would* come out. Another month or so and she'd be showing. Her family would ask questions, they'd speculate and she knew it wouldn't be long before they worked it out.

And Scott had a right to know he was about to become a father before the rest of the world did. Only...she wasn't sure how to do it.

Over the following days she picked up the telephone a dozen times and started emails she didn't send. But how did she tell him something like that? Especially when their fledgling relationship was over and all that remained was a courteous, forced friendship held together because they were now obscurely related by the marriage of their siblings.

So, as the days morphed into a week, and then another, her courage dwindled. Evie knew she was living in a vacuum of borrowed time. Trevor kept asking her what was wrong. So did her mother and Noah.

Physically she felt good. The nausea was gone, and her appetite had resumed with a vengeance. She remembered her wanton addiction to toffee ice cream when she'd been pregnant with Trevor, and this time appeared to be no different. She had her first appointment with her obstetrician and scheduled a time to have her first ultrasound the following month.

And still she didn't tell Scott. In fact, she'd been so preoccupied with not telling him, she hadn't responded to any of his emails for a couple of weeks.

In March she received another email.

March 15
I haven't heard from you lately. Is everything okay? Scott.

Evie stared at the computer screen and fought the urge to hit the delete button. But she didn't.

March 24
I'm fine.

March 25
Trevor said you've been sick again? I'm worried about you. What's wrong?

She deliberated for an hour. But she knew it was time for the truth. He had rights and she had an obligation to tell him what was happening. They'd both made love that night, and her resulting pregnancy was a shared responsibility. Whatever Scott chose to do with the information was up to him. All Evie knew was that she wanted the baby. She wanted this precious gift more than she'd ever dared imagine. She took a deep breath and wrote.

March 26
I'm pregnant.

Chapter Twelve

Scott wandered around his apartment that night, barefoot, in jeans and a worn T-shirt; he walked from room to room, trying to soothe the crushing ache behind his ribs.

A baby...

Evie was having his baby. But he felt as if he'd been punched in the gut. That she would tell him like that...it seemed so outrageously callous he could barely get his head around it. And Evie wasn't callous. Of course, he knew she was notoriously hardheaded about some things... but he couldn't believe she would send an email containing two words and think that was adequate.

Scott headed for the kitchen and grabbed a beer from the refrigerator.

His head felt as if it were about to explode. He gulped some beer, winced as the cold liquid froze his brain for a few seconds and tried his best to be as mad as hell at Evie.

But no use. He'd spent months in a kind of dazed

limbo—missing her, wanting her so much he couldn't think about anything else. He'd gone back to work and gone through the motions, determined to keep his head because he knew what the consequences could be if he let the distraction take hold of him.

But the nights were impossible. He hurt all over just thinking about Evie.

I'm going to be a father.

And he didn't quite know what he felt. Shock, definitely. And fear. And the absolute certainty that he wanted to share this child with Evie. And not just as a distant, absent parent. But how could it work? His life was in L.A.… Evie's was in Crystal Point.

He dropped his half-empty bottle into the trash and walked back into the living room. The laptop still sat on the coffee table in the center of the room. He should call her. Scott picked up the telephone, thinking of her number that he couldn't remember memorizing but somehow had. The telephone stuck to his hand. What would he say— *Thanks for the news…let me know when our kid arrives?* Yeah, as if that was gonna happen.

The doorbell rang and he shook himself. A few seconds later three of his friends piled into his apartment, carrying six-packs of Bud and pizza boxes.

"The game's on, remember?" Clint Dawson reminded him as he stood as if he were a statue and let them pass. "And you're the one with the big flat screen."

The game? Flat screen? Right…he vaguely remembered agreeing to an evening in with his friends, sharing the tab for takeout and watching the game on TV.

He shut the door and watched Clint, and then Marcus Crane, drop into the pair of recliners that had prime position in front of the flat screen. Gabe Vitali, his first cousin and closest friend, was the only one of the trio who thought to ask him if he was all right. Scott only shrugged, thinking the last thing he wanted was a night in with his friends. He wanted to get his thoughts together. He wanted to speak with Evie, to hear her voice, to tell her what he felt...

Which was what, exactly?

The constant ache in his chest, the lack of pleasure he got from doing anything, the almost robotic way he'd been living since he left her...what did that mean? And what they'd had together felt like more than he'd experienced before...more feeling...more passion...more everything.

He looked at his friends—newly divorced Clint, commitment-phobic Marcus and his cousin, whose fiancée had run off the year Gabe had been diagnosed with a serious illness. What did any of them have beyond the job and an apartment? Scott felt the meaninglessness of his existence through to the marrow in his bones.

And now Evie was having his baby. He wanted to shout it to the world. The shock had dissipated and was replaced by a sense of calm so acute it felt almost euphoric. Suddenly, like a shard of glass striking through his blood, Scott knew what he wanted.

Everything. Evie—the baby—a life scratching at his fingertips.

He wanted Evie. He wanted their baby. Nothing else mattered.

He stalked across the room and grabbed the remote, then flicked off the TV and turned to face his startled friends.

"I'm in love," he announced, watching as three broad jaws dropped. "And I'm going to be a dad."

Evie covered herself in the baggiest smock she could find, hiding itself in the archives of her old maternity wardrobe. At four months along she was really beginning to show. For the past few weeks she had managed to avoid too many interactions with her family and friends—but she knew she couldn't keep up the pretense forever. Especially to Trevor. Being a hermit would last only so long. Her mother wouldn't be held at bay for too much longer. Grace was calling her every few days. And Fiona was doing what friends do by trying to leech the truth from her. Her family would come around, mob fashion if need be, and she had to be prepared for the onslaught. They would mean well, but they would also demand answers to questions she was not prepared to consider.

Okay, so her pregnancy would be revealing itself to the world soon. But she had no intention of admitting anything about her baby's paternity until she spoke to Scott again. And he hadn't communicated with her at all.

Too apprehensive to email him again, or call, she caged herself into her house like a hibernating bear. And as the cold fingers of doubt climbed over every inch of skin with each passing day, Evie convinced herself that telling Scott about the baby was the worst thing she could have done.

He obviously doesn't care one way or another. And it hurt. It hurt so much she could barely stand thinking about it. And it wasn't that she had any kind of expectations— she simply couldn't believe he'd drop contact altogether.

So she was to be a single mother. Wasn't that what she'd planned anyway? From the moment she'd discovered she was pregnant, Evie had known she would be going it alone. And she was fine with that. Perfectly fine. She'd been a single mother for ten years, after all.

Only…she remembered those first precious moments when Trevor was born…she remembered the look in Gordon's eyes, the tears of pride and wonderment toward the new and perfect life they had created together. Evie instinctively placed her hands on her growing belly, and a hot surge of love washed over her. *I'll love you,* she promised her baby. *I'll love you and keep you safe.*

Without Scott. Besides, he was only her temporary lover and someone she shouldn't have fallen in love with. The fact that she had was her burden to bear. He'd broken no promises to her. He was too young…too much the kind of man she didn't want in her life and a risk she could never take. Especially now that she had a new baby to consider.

She would get on with her life, as she had always done. And once her family knew, she was certain they would support her decision to raise her child alone. Besides, nothing could dampen her joy at being pregnant. She was happy.

It was three days later that the downstairs doorbell woke her up from her usual afternoon nap. Evie checked her watch and clambered off the bed. Two o'clock. She remembered that Noah was coming around to hang a few of her paintings in the downstairs living room. To be *really* painting again had been a surprise—but strangely, her passion had returned with a vengeance. She had finished a few pieces she'd started years before, ever mindful of the small crystal globe and Saint Catherine watching over her from its spot on a shelf near her easels.

And maybe she would tell her brother about the pregnancy. She'd always been able to share things with Noah. They'd been there for one another over the years—when his wife had walked out on him and the kids, when Gordon had died, when Trevor had needed a father's influence. Evie trusted her brother with her news.

Evie reached the door and flung it back wide on its hinges. "You're two hours early," she complained with a laugh as she flipped open the security screen. "And you interrupted my afternoon—"

She stopped and caught her words in her throat. It

wasn't her brother standing on her doorstep. It was the father of her baby.

Scott's gaze dropped instantly to her belly. He lingered there for a moment and she heard him suck in a sharp breath. "Hello, Evie."

She took a step backward. "What are you doing here?"

"You really have to ask that?" he replied as he met her eyes. "I want to talk to you."

Evie absorbed everything about him in a second—the jeans and cotton Henley he wore so well, the duffel at his feet, the way his hair flopped over his forehead, the travel-weary look on his face. Her insides lurched and she instinctively laid her hands on her stomach. "I...I—"

"Can I come in?"

She took a second, thought about all the reasons why she shouldn't let him inside and couldn't come up with a single one. "Of course."

He grabbed his bag and walked across the threshold. Evie headed for the living room and sat down on the sofa. She gripped her hands together and waited. Scott stood by the doorway and dropped his duffel. A few seconds past and he moved toward her. Evie got a good look at him and noticed he'd lost weight. There was a ranginess about his lean frame and she wondered if perhaps she was responsible for it. His eyes were dark, like the color of an indigo sky. And his mouth was pressed into a thin line. He looked so tired. She touched her stomach and saw his gaze immediately follow the movement of her hands.

"Scott, I—"

"How could you do it?" he demanded, running a hand through his hair. "How could you tell me like that?"

Evie choked back a gasp. He wasn't tired, she realized. He was angry. "I can—"

"Two words," he said, throwing his hands up. "Two

words to announce the most important thing that's ever been said to me."

"I'm sorry," she said quickly, feeling the bite of shame snap at her heels. She *was* in the wrong, and they both knew it. "You're right. I shouldn't have told you like that. I should have called you and told you about the baby."

Scott let out a breath and turned, then paced across the room until he reached the window. His back was straight and Evie knew him well enough to recognize the tension searing through his body. He took a few long breaths and stared out the window for a moment before finally twisting around to look at her.

"So, how are you?" he asked, clearly back in control now. "I mean…how's the… How are you feeling?"

Evie patted her stomach. "I'm good," she replied softly. "*We're* good."

"You've been ill?"

She shook her head. "Just the normal pregnancy things."

He expelled an exasperated breath. "Well, considering this is my first experience with pregnancy, you might consider being a bit more specific."

"Nausea," she explained a little stiffly. "And fatigue. And my doctor is keeping an eye on my blood sugar, considering my age. Other than that I feel fine. The baby is healthy and growing normally. I had my first scan last week—I have a picture if you like."

He looked as if she'd slapped him in the face and she knew immediately how exclusive and selfish it sounded. She wanted to explain to him how she'd felt seeing their baby on the screen for the first time, how her heart had constricted so tight with love and joy and how she'd longed to share the moment with him but had thought it impossible.

"A picture?" he echoed softly. "And do you know…" He

paused and swallowed hard. Evie watched his throat move up and down. "Do you know the baby's sex?"

She shook her head. "I wanted it to be a surprise. If you're keen to find out, I can schedule another ultrasound."

"I'm happy to wait. But I would like to come with you next time."

"Of course," she whispered. "So, you're staying for a while?"

He nodded. "I'm staying. Have you told anyone?" he asked. "Your family?"

"No. Although I don't imagine I'll be able to keep it a secret for too much longer. I think they're all suspicious about why I've been avoiding them for the past few weeks."

He looked at her stomach. "You're already showing."

Evie spread the cotton smock across her abdomen. "Yes. I'd like to tell Trevor—and my parents."

"We'll do it together."

Evie wasn't sure what to think. He looked so far away, still angry but fighting it. She felt like caving in and crawling into his arms. But she had to keep her head. "That's not necessary. I can do it alone."

"Yeah," he said quickly. "I'm sure you can. But you're not alone, Evie," he said, and pointed to her belly. "You're not alone in this."

But she'd felt alone. For weeks she'd felt like the only person on the planet. "But you didn't respond to my message," she said on a shallow breath. "I thought…I thought you didn't…"

"You thought I didn't what?"

Emotion clogged her throat. "I thought you didn't want… I didn't hear from you, so I assumed you—"

"It's hardly the thing to be discussed in an email," he said, cutting her off. "Or over the telephone."

"But for the past two weeks—"

"For the past two weeks I've been organizing extended leave from my job and subletting my apartment."

She stilled. What did that mean? He was here, but for how long? And what kind of role did he want to play during her pregnancy? And afterward? What then? Would he expect shared custody of the child they had made together?

"Why have you done that?"

He gave her an odd look. "You can't be serious?" He shook his head. "You're having a baby, Evie...my baby... What did you expect me to do, hang out in L.A. until the kid was born and then send you flowers?"

"I'm not sure what I expected," she said frankly. "Nothing really. Only for you to know. I haven't really thought that far ahead."

"Well, you need to think about it. *We* need to think about it."

He came across the room and sat beside her and took her hands in his. Evie didn't move. She couldn't feel anything other than the strong clasp of his fingers against her own. "I want...I want this baby, Scott," she said in a shaky voice.

His grip tightened. "So do I."

Hot tears burned behind her eyes. "I'm glad. And you can see as much of the baby as you like for as long as you're here."

He shook her hands. "Evie," he said rawly. "You don't understand. I don't want to be a part-time parent." He turned on the seat and dropped to his knees onto the floor in front of her. "I said I was staying and I meant it. I want... I want to make this right. I want us to raise our child together."

Dazed, Evie shook her head. "Together? What do you—"

"Marry me?"

The room tilted and she swayed, leaning forward. Scott

grasped her shoulders and set her upright. She still spun, she still felt as if the carpet beneath her feet were moving from side to side, pulling her with it. *Marry me?* Evie sucked in a breath as the fingers of temptation entwined around her heart. Marry the man she was in love with? The man whose child she carried? It seemed like a dream come true.

Yes...a dream. A fantasy. Evie knew better than to rely on dreams. She had to rely on her good sense. On what was best for her baby. Marrying a much younger man who was a firefighter made no sense at all.

"No," she whispered.

He paled. "No?"

Evie shook her head. "You don't have to marry me, Scott. You can see the baby. I won't deny you the right to be a father."

"What about my right to be your husband and lover?"

She pulled her hands from his and straightened. "Look, I appreciate that you want to do the honorable thing. But you're too young for me, Scott. We're like...we're from two completely different generations."

"It's nine years, Evie—not twenty. And even if it were, I wouldn't care." He reached up and held her face against his palms. "I love you."

Evie's heart skipped a beat, and then another. *He loves me?* Could he? Or was he simply saying that to get what he wanted? Part of her longed to believe it...longed to say yes. But Sensible Evie stuck out her neck. "We hardly know each other."

He touched her stomach, and her whole body shook. "We do know each other, Evie. Intimately. And I know that I'm in love with you."

Rocked to the core by his revelation, Evie placed her

hand on his. "It's lust, Scott—desire. And maybe some sense of obligation because of the baby."

He jumped to his feet. "You're telling me what I feel?"

Evie shrugged, feeling the loss of his hands on her. "I'm just trying to let you off the hook."

"And what if I don't want to be let off?" he asked. "What if I want to be joined to you for the rest of my life?"

"Because of the baby?"

"Because I'm head over heels in love with you, that's why." He took her hands and gently eased her to her feet. "Evie…give us a chance?"

Doubt swirled through her. She couldn't do it. "There's too much against it working. The age difference…your job…"

"I'll quit," he announced, and wrapped his arms around her.

Evie moved against him. "You can't do that," she protested. "I wouldn't allow it."

He shrugged. "It's not your decision. I'll quit and find another job—here. Because wherever you are, Evie, is where I want to be."

She pulled back. "You're a firefighter. That's what you do. It's who you are."

"It's a job."

She shook her head and stepped away, determined to keep him at an arm's length. "I saw you, Scott—I saw you with the volunteers that day. I saw the way you were with those people, the way they responded to you. I knew then that your job was more than merely a job to you. It's part of you…it's part of the man you are. You love it."

"I love you more," he said simply.

Evie touched her belly. "Maybe right now, right here, when you see me carrying your child and look into my eyes and know I'm just as…that my feelings for you are just as strong."

His eyes widened. "Are they, Evie? Do you love me?"

Evie took a step back. "Loving you isn't the issue. The issue is marrying you…and I won't do it." She crossed her arms and inhaled deeply. "I'm tired. I need to rest for a bit. You can sleep in your old room or down here if you prefer, as I have no guests at the moment. You can stay until we sort something out."

"There's nothing to sort out," he said. "I've told you what I want…and in this, Evie, there can be no compromise."

She nodded. "I agree. I won't marry you. The sooner you accept that, the better."

And then Evie pulled on all her strength and walked out of the room.

As rejections went, Scott thought, this was pretty well up there. Back in his old room, he could barely look at the bed without imagining Evie in it.

Nice going, dude…nothing like a marriage proposal that sounded more like an ultimatum.

Did she love him? Had her roundabout admission actually been real? If she'd refused him because she didn't care enough, how did he get through that? He wanted to marry Evie. He wanted to be her husband and lover and protector. He wanted her love. And she hadn't exactly said she did. There were feelings there, he was sure of it. Evie was an honest, sincere woman, and not the kind of person to fake what she felt. And he *felt* love from her when they were together. And she *made love* to him as though she loved him.

He looked out the window. A car pulled up outside and he watched a pretty redhead get out. Evie's friend—

again he couldn't remember her name—locked her car and waited by the curb. Seconds later another vehicle pulled up. He recognized his sister and brother-in-law immediately.

Great. Annoyance waved up his spine. He wondered for a moment if Callie had sniffed out his arrival with her sister-radar—but he'd only told his cousin Gabe and his mother his plans and had sworn Eleanor to secrecy. This horde was obviously about Evie. He remembered how weary she'd looked and knew visitors would be the last thing she wanted. The trio came down the path and Scott watched them disappear beneath the eaves. He heard voices downstairs, heard feet walking across the threshold.

He didn't waste a second more and left the room. When he got downstairs and entered the kitchen, he felt as if he'd walked into the middle of a gunslinger's stand-off. Callie was frowning, the redhead was staring with wide eyes and hopping on her feet and Noah looked like a man who wanted answers. Only Evie appeared calm. She stood by the sink, hands on hips.

"I'm not sick," Scott heard her say as he rounded the doorway. "So stop worrying."

"We *are* worried," Noah said gravely. "You've been hiding out here for weeks now. You won't talk to anyone, you won't see anyone, you won't admit that something serious is going on with you. Our mother is convinced you've—"

"I'm not sick," she said again, and quickly spotted Scott as he framed the entry. Three sets of eyes snapped toward him instantly. "I'm pregnant."

The trio all did a good impression of a rabbit stuck in headlights.

Callie stared at him, her surprise obvious. He probably should have called his sister and told her he was coming. But right now his priority was Evie.

Callie said his name and then quickly clammed up. She

looked at Evie, and then back to Scott, then Evie again. It took only seconds for his sister to figure it out. The other two responded a little slower, but when they did emotion charged through the room.

"Pregnant?" Noah echoed incredulously.

"Well!" the redhead exclaimed. "Aren't you one for secrets?"

"It's not a secret, Fiona," Evie said evenly. "We chose to maintain our privacy, that's all."

We? Scott almost laughed. But now was not the time to challenge Evie. They needed a united front. "So I guess the interrogation's over?"

Callie moved across the room and grabbed his arm. "Not by a long shot. You've got some serious explaining to do."

Scott smiled at his feisty sister. "That's hardly appropriate," he said, and saw Noah glaring at him. "Besides, we're not teenagers. And we're not trying to hide anything. We're having a baby together and as long as we're okay with that it doesn't really matter what anyone else thinks."

He looked at Evie and saw the barest traces of relief on her face. Whatever he had to do to prove to her he was determined to make it work he would do. He'd beg and plead if he had to, to make her see sense, to make her realize what they had…what they could have together if only she'd let him into her life. He wanted to be a father to their baby…but he wanted Evie, too. He wanted her love. And he'd do whatever was necessary to get it.

"So, while you're all here for this intervention," he said, and chucked his hands into his pockets, "maybe you can all use your influence and convince Evie to marry me."

Chapter Thirteen

It was a low act. A despicable, humiliating thing to do. And Evie was so mad she seethed. She banged things around the house for the next hour, after quietly asking her family to leave. They hadn't wanted to leave at first and Callie looked as if she was ready to kill her brother.

Noah and Fiona had been a little less disapproving, with Noah saying he thought marriage was a great idea. *A great idea?* Evie had burned her brother with a red-hot glare for being so agreeable. She'd looked at Scott and he'd just shrugged and smiled and showed off that dimple.

Well, she wasn't falling for that sexy dimple and gorgeous smile anymore.

He was outside shooting hoops with Trevor—who'd been so pleased to see him when he'd arrived home from school that Evie had swallowed a lump the size of a tennis ball as her son had embraced Scott. Considering Evie had made it abundantly clear she wanted to be alone, they'd left her immediately.

So she had thinking time while she rearranged the pot drawer in the downstairs kitchen. She wouldn't be maneuvered into a corner, that was for sure. And she wouldn't marry Scott because it was what everyone else wanted.

But when a pair of skinny hands landed on her shoulders a short while later, Evie felt her resistance crumble fractionally.

"Scott told me," Trevor said quietly. "About everything."

Evie turned around and saw her son look at her stomach. "He did?"

Trevor shrugged. "I'm okay about the baby. And Scott said he's hanging around—which is good, too." Her son squeezed her arm and shuffled back on his feet. "And I reckon it'll be cool to have a stepfather."

Evie's temper surged and she wondered if Scott would be so duplicitous to use her hero-worshipping son to get her to change her mind. He wouldn't, surely? "I'm glad you and Scott get along so well."

"Families are supposed to, aren't they?"

"Yes," she replied, but didn't point out that Scott wasn't exactly family.

"And having a new baby might get you to stop treating me like a little kid?"

He was grinning, but Evie saw through his smile. "Do I? I don't mean to."

He shrugged lightly. "I know. But sometimes, when you want to know where I am every second and try to hand-pick my friends, it gets hard to take."

She took a step back and leaned against the counter. "Is that what I do?" Evie considered her son's words. "I didn't realize I was being so overprotective."

Trevor shrugged again. "It's okay. I get why you do it.

But you know, when I might want to hang out with some of my friends, even the ones you don't like all that much, I reckon you should let me make my own decision."

It seemed like a huge leap for Evie. Her son was no longer a little boy. He was growing up so fast and she didn't want to let him go.

"You know," Trevor said as he grabbed an apple from the fruit bowl, "I like Scott. I vote we keep him."

She stared after him as he left the room and was about to return to her chore of banging pots when Scott came through the doorway. She scowled at him. "Being underhanded won't get you anywhere."

He rested one shoulder against the jamb. "What does that mean?"

Eve straightened. "My son, who obviously believes you can do no wrong, told me he thinks we should keep you."

"He's a smart kid," Scott said, straight-faced.

Evie raised her brows dramatically. "He is smart. But he's easily influenced. I'd prefer it if you kept our relationship private."

"I didn't say anything about *our relationship,* Evie," he said. "I only told him about the baby."

She scowled. "I *did* intend to tell him."

"Of course you did. But, I *needed* to tell Trevor myself, man to man," he said, and pushed off the jamb. "If I overstepped the mark, I'm sorry."

It *was* a little presumptuous, she thought. "How did he take the news?"

Scott shrugged. "He was surprised at first," Scott told her quietly as he made his way around the countertop. "And he asked me about my intentions." He smiled. "But I think he understands. He's a smart kid. A good kid. You've done a great job raising him, Evie. If I'm half the parent you are, I'll be a happy man."

Evie fought the heat behind her eyes and pressed her hips against the bench. "Sometimes I forget he won't be a child for much longer. He's growing up. So, thank you for explaining it to him." He chuckled and Evie frowned. "What's funny?"

"Nothing," Scott replied as he moved into the kitchen. "But I think we both just agreed on how to parent a teenager."

It surprised her. It also surprised her that suddenly she didn't actually mind Scott running interference with Trevor. "I guess we'll have plenty of practice soon enough."

Scott was in front of her now. He reached out and placed his hand across her belly. "Do you mind?" he asked softly.

Evie shook her head. "Of course not."

"Can you feel the baby moving?"

She smiled. "Not quite moving," she replied. "More like fluttering, I suppose you'd call it. Another month or so and it will be a different story. When I was pregnant with Trevor I felt like I had a soccer player inside me."

Scott raised his brows. "Do girls play soccer?"

"Are you hoping for a girl?"

He rubbed her stomach gently. "I thought you might prefer it."

Evie felt the heat from his touch rise over her skin like a bloom. "I'm happy either way."

His touch changed slightly, shifting to something that reminded her of how it was to be made love to by this man. But she didn't pull away. His hand trailed around her hip and up her side, lingering on the underswell of her breast.

"Your breasts are bigger," he said, and moved closer.

Evie colored, good sense tugging at her wits. Only, it was useless to imagine she could pull away. "Of course."

"There's no 'of course' for me," he said, and traced the back of his hand across one nipple. "This is all new...your body changing…the incredible way you look even more beautiful, if that were possible."

"I'm not beautiful."

"You are to me."

Evie swayed. "Don't do this," she pleaded. "Don't use my attraction for you against me."

His expression narrowed. "Evie," he said softly as he grasped her chin. "Sometimes you say the damnedest things."

"I don't want to confuse the lines here, Scott. I want to stay clear about what I need to do."

He released her abruptly. "You mean by refusing to marry me?"

Evie pushed herself along the countertop. "You know why I won't."

"I do?" He stepped back. "That's news to me. I don't get you at all, Evie. We have this unbelievable opportunity to be a part of something great together. But you won't even consider meeting me halfway."

She bristled and snapped out the first thing she thought of. "You're too young for me."

"That's an old song," he said. "But if it bothers you so much I'll dye my hair gray and spend loads of time in the sun so I wrinkle up by the time I'm forty."

"And I'll be nearly fifty," she reminded him. "You'll still be gorgeous and I'll be a middle-age, menopausal wreck. You'll have younger women chasing after you and I won't have a hope of competing with them."

"That's ridiculous. And I don't believe for one minute that you're that insecure."

"I am," she announced, wishing she was a better actress. She wrapped her arms around her chest and expelled a heavy breath. "This is such a disaster."

He quickly took three steps back and shook his head as

he glanced at her belly. "I'm gonna forget you said that."
He rubbed a hand over his face. "I'm also going to hit the
sack because the jet lag is kicking in and I feel like hell.
But I'll see you later and we'll talk some more."

She watched him leave and sank back against the counter. *What am I going to do?* Having Scott so close wreaked
havoc on her good sense. With an ocean between them
she'd felt stronger, as though she could do it alone. But this
was like being a kid and browsing through a candy store,
where everything was so close, but locked beneath a glass
cabinet. She was the sugar-addicted kid, and Scott was the
candy. Wanting him…longing for him in ways she never
imagined she'd want any man again. It made her feel exposed and vulnerable.

Evie didn't see Scott again until the following morning. When he entered the upstairs kitchen, she'd already
pushed Trevor out the door for school and refreshed the
lavender bedroom for the guests who were arriving the
following day.

He loped into the room in low-flung loose fitting jeans
and a red T-shirt and helped himself to coffee. "Good
morning."

Evie stalked across the room and sat down at the table.
"You wanted to talk," she said, determined to be practical. "Okay, let's talk. First, how long are you staying?"

He sat down opposite her. "Is that a trick question?"

"What?"

Scott put down his mug. "Well, if I say I'm staying forever you'll give me one of your disapproving looks and
tell me it's never gonna happen. But if I say I'm here tem-
porarily, you'll hit me with how you'd expect nothing less
from me than if I abandoned you and the baby."

Evie's spine jerked upward. "I wouldn't say that."

Scott raised a brow. "Really? What would you say, then?"

"I don't see the point of—"

"For good, Evie," he said quietly. "I might have to go back to hand in my resignation and put my apartment on the market. But I can't see that taking too long. My parents made sure Callie and I had dual residency since we were kids. I can live here or the States."

"And then?"

"And then I'll get a job so I can support you and the baby."

"I can support myself," she pointed out. "As I have done for the last ten years. The B and B is lucrative enough and I recently sold a few paintings."

"You're painting again?"

Evie nodded. "Yes. My muse is back."

"So your heart isn't broken anymore?"

She gripped her teacup. "Not like it was."

He pushed his mug into the center of the table and stood. "Good. Because I want your heart, Evie, and I'll do whatever it takes to get it. And I fully intend to support you and our baby, and be a stepdad and friend to Trevor. So get used to me being around. Get used to being loved. I'm not going anywhere."

Evie's heart lurched forward. "You can't stay here…I can't do this. I won't be manipulated into—"

"I have no desire to manipulate the mother of my child. But I know you're running scared, Evie. And I'm not sure why."

"You think everything's black-and-white," she said statically. "Nothing's that simple. You said you're going to quit your job with the LAFD and look for work over here. But as what, a firefighter?"

"I haven't—"

"Of course it will be," she said, her heart and body filled with so much pain and fear she could barely get the words out. "That's what you do…that's who you are. You'll join the fire department here and keep running into those buildings and the only difference will be geography. And I know I don't have any right to ask you to be someone other than who you are. You *are* a firefighter. And maybe for a little while you could try doing something else, but we both know your heart wouldn't be in it."

He looked at her and there was raw truth in his eyes. "I'd sweep streets for you, Evie."

"But you'd be unhappy," she said. "And because of that you'd be distracted. It would be like your friend Mike all over again. You'd be distracted and I'd be worried sick every time you left the house, every time I heard the sirens wailing." Evie stood up and pushed her chair back, fighting the tears batting against her lashes. "And then one day, something would happen, and you'd get injured…or maybe worse…and our child might be left without a father…and I'd…and I'd be left without…and I can't…"

She stopped speaking and closed her eyes. It was harder than hard. But she needed to say it. She needed to hear herself say the words.

The admission came out as a whisper as tears fell. "I just don't have the strength to bury another husband."

Scott moved out of Dunn Inn that afternoon. Evie didn't know where he went and she didn't ask before he drove off in his rental car. She had her life back. Sort of.

But true to his word, he didn't abandon her.

In fact, he became a permanent fixture in her daily routine over the following week.

At first he dropped by to see how she was doing, and not once did he repeat his marriage proposal. He hung out with Trevor some afternoons and at other times discussed the baby, or when they'd start decorating the upstairs guest room into a nursery. They talked colors and wallpaper and booster seats and cribs and pretty much everything to do with the baby and nothing about their relationship.

She should have been happy about it.

Instead she became more miserable with each day. He didn't touch her, didn't try to kiss her and didn't do anything even remotely intimate. He just talked. When he wasn't talking he was doing things around the B and B. He fixed anything she asked to be repaired and didn't voice one complaint.

At her parents' house one Sunday to celebrate her father's birthday, Evie prepared herself to endure the scrutiny of her family's curiosity about their relationship. But their *relationship* had developed into something so *lukewarm* it barely rated mentioning. More to the point, no one seemed to care. She was pregnant; Scott was the father of her baby. Even her mother, who would normally be gushing over the idea that one of her daughters was in a relationship, even if a slightly dysfunctional one, only smiled and patted her shoulder and mentioned what a nice man he was and how she was looking forward to being a grandmother again.

Nice...sure...more like a wolf in sheep's clothing.

And that was exactly how she felt. As if his indifference was deliberate. Her declarations about fearing something might happen to him had clearly struck a chord with him and he'd backed off. Or at least that's what he wanted her to think. Yeah—some disguises were used for camouflage and some for hunting. Evie wasn't fooled. He was on the hunt...and she was the prey.

Scott had said he didn't want to manipulate her. But she felt manipulated.

And by Sunday afternoon she was a mass of nervous energy, waiting for him to pounce. She would rather have met him head-on and deal with his marriage proposal and the attraction they had for each other than play this waiting game.

Fortunately, Evie found an ally in her sister. Grace was back from New York for a few days for the party, and Evie was grateful for her sister's support.

"You know he's staying with Hot Tub, don't you?" Grace told her, sitting down to share the love seat by the pool, which Evie had occupied for the past lazy hour because it was sheltered and quiet and away from Scott, who was playing pool with her brother and Trevor. Her sister handed her a long glass of iced tea.

Hot Tub. Cameron Jakowski. It made her grin. Grace and Cameron loathed each other, and their private war had been going on for years. The ultracharming police officer was the only person Evie had ever known who was able to ruffle Grace's supercool composure.

"I didn't know that," Evie admitted. "But we're not exactly talking about things that matter at the moment."

"No more declarations of love?" Grace inquired.

"Not one." She'd told her sister what had transpired between them in the eighteen hours he'd stayed at the B and B.

"Are you in love with him?" Grace asked frankly. "I mean, besides being full of hormones and the emotions tied up with being pregnant with his baby. Do you actually *love* him?"

"Yes," she whispered.

"And that's not enough?"

"Logically it is," Evie replied as she drank some tea. "But I'm afraid of who I'll become if I let myself go there."

Grace tutted and tapped her perfectly manicured nails

together. "And I thought I was the closed-off neurotic in the family."

"I don't think there's any doubt about that, *Princess*."

They snapped their necks around instantly. Cameron stood by the pool fence, beer in hand. He smiled at them both and raised his drink in salute.

"What do you want, Hot Tub?"

He grinned. "To see what a five-hundred-dollar pair of shoes look like."

Evie immediately looked to Grace's feet and the Jimmy Choo sandals she wore.

Grace stood and glared at him. Evie watched as her sister gave Cameron a murderous look and then took off back to the house. "You know," Evie said, "one day you're going to go too far and she'll come at you in all her fury."

He chuckled. "I look forward to it."

"Don't say I didn't warn you."

Cameron laughed again and asked Evie if she needed anything before he returned to the games room. Evie languished beneath the Balinese-style hut overlooking the pool and closed her eyes for a moment.

"If you fall asleep in that chair you'll get a back cramp."

Her lids fluttered open. Scott had approached with all the stealth of a leopard. "I'll have a spa when I get home to take the kinks out."

His eyes darkened. "Be careful getting in and out of the tub."

"Are you offering your assistance?" she asked, smiling.

Scott sucked in a breath. "I'm saying be careful you don't slip and hurt yourself."

"I won't," she said. "I have no intention of doing anything that might harm the baby."

He looked at her with blistering intensity. "Me, either."

Clarity washed over Evie like a wave. "Of course—

that explains the Mr. Nice Guy act you've had going all week." She pulled herself straight in the seat and then stood up. "I'm not fooled by it. And I'd rather you simply be yourself."

He shrugged. "I don't want to upset you."

"Too late," she snapped. "Do you think talking about teddy-bear wallpaper and prenatal vitamins are such neutral subjects that I won't be tempted to burst into tears and act like a hormonal lunatic?"

Scott stared at her and shook his head. "I can't do anything right with you, can I?"

"I'm only—"

"Your way or no way," he said stiffly. "And no way in between."

Evie bristled. "That's not true."

"It is true. There's no middle road with you and it's so damned frustrating." The air around him was filled with pent-up emotion so powerful Evie could only watch, fascinated and mesmerized. "I asked to be your husband and you turned me down... I'm trying to be your friend and that's not good enough. The only place I've ever felt marginally welcome in your life is between the sheets...and that...and that just...kills me."

Evie gasped. "Scott, I—"

He reached for her and took hold of her shoulders, molding her bones with his big hands. "Is that what you want from me?" he demanded, and Evie was suddenly so turned on, so hungry for him and so ashamed to admit it she could hardly draw breath. "Is that all you want from me?" His body was hard against hers and he stared down into her upturned face. "Just this?" One hand swept down her back to cover her behind and urge her closer. "Is that really all this is to you?"

Before she could say a word his mouth came down on

hers. It was hot and hard and had ownership stamped all over it. But Evie didn't mind and shocked herself by kissing him back hungrily.

"No," she said when he was done, when their breathing was ragged and their mouths were finally apart.

He released her gently. "But it's not enough for you to marry me, right? I know you're scared, Evie... I know you think I'm gonna die on the job and leave you. And you know what—maybe that will happen. Because there are no guarantees in any relationship. But if you can't get past that fear and keep refusing to marry me and let me take care of you and all we'll share together is that baby inside you—then, that's okay. Because that in itself is an incredible thing."

He stepped back, took a long breath and then left her alone without another word.

"You look like hell."

Scott jerked his gaze upward. He was sitting in Cameron Jakowski's living room, and Cameron and Noah were loafing back in a pair of recliners. He felt their scrutiny and shrugged. "Whatever."

And his brother-in-law was probably right. He felt like crap and figured he probably looked worse.

"Are you sleeping?" Noah asked, and grabbed the remote from Cameron. He flicked off the motor sports program none of them were watching.

"Not much," he admitted, and suddenly felt like spilling his guts to these two men who had quickly become friends. "Who knew, huh?" he said, and laughed at himself. "That it would feel this bad," he explained when he saw Cameron frown.

Noah looked heavenward. "I did."

Scott grinned. "Yeah—I guess my sister put you though the wringer a few months back."

"And then some," Noah said, and looked as if he was thinking stuff Scott was certain he didn't want to know about his sister. "But it was definitely worth it."

"Schmucks," Cameron said, looking mildly appalled.

"He thinks he's immune," Noah explained, grinning. "I keep telling him the harder the resistance, the bigger the fall."

"Not likely," Cameron replied. "I don't ever want to have that pathetic hangdog look on my face. Next you pair will be wanting a group hug." He scowled and took a long swallow of Corona. "Forget it."

Scott laughed. "I'm good," he insisted, and then a sharp pain pierced his chest when he realized he could certainly do with a hug from Evie. He'd backed off to give her space and felt the loss of her so acutely it was messing with his head. But he didn't want to upset her and was worried what anxiety might do to their baby. So he stayed away and endured the longest five days of his life.

And he was angry with her, too. Angry that she was afraid to give them a chance. Angry that she didn't *want* to love him. It...hurt. He'd never felt hurt like that before... never knew that pain like that could stop a man eating, sleeping, almost breathing.

"She'll come around," Noah said. "I know Evie. She's set in her ways about some things...but she's the most sensible person I know. And she's been on her own for so long. Give her some time."

"Well, I've got plenty of that."

"Schmucks," Cameron said again just as his cell phone pealed. He headed off down the hall to get the call and returned a few minutes later.

"That was one of my boys from the Big Brother program," he told them. "Giving me the heads-up. Apparently there's some trouble going down at the surf club tonight." He grabbed his keys as Scott and Noah got to their feet. "Teenagers fighting over turf."

A turf war in Crystal Point? It seemed incomprehensible. "Do you know these kids?"

"Yeah," Cameron replied. "Some of them. One group has been using the top floor for secret computer gaming parties. They weren't doing any harm, so we've let them use the place while the renovations are going on. The other group wants them out. I don't want to call it in until I know something's really going on. I gotta go."

"I'll come with you," Scott said.

Noah nodded. "Me, too."

Cameron looked at them both. "And you might want to decide if you should call Evie," he said. "Because my source told me that Trevor was there with them."

Chapter Fourteen

Evie taught her Friday night class with about as much enthusiasm as a wet sneaker. Callie had turned up for the class, with Noah's three youngest kids in tow, and the kids played happily with watercolors at their specially set up table in the corner.

Once the class had concluded, Fiona and Callie lingered in the studio drinking a second cup of coffee and Evie prepared herself for what she knew was an inevitable confrontation with her sister-in-law.

"Have you guys picked out names yet?" Callie asked over the rim of her mug.

"Not yet. But I'm thinking I'd like a family name and something traditional."

Callie nodded. "And the baby's surname," she asked, "what will that be?"

Evie stilled. The implication was clear. "We haven't really discussed it."

"Scott intends to be a hands-on parent," Callie said. "He'll be a good father."

Evie didn't doubt that for a moment. "I know."

"The thing is," Callie said as she flicked a look toward Fiona and then back to Evie. "He's always been… you know…rock-solid. When we were growing up I was always this unpredictable whirlwind, and Scott was exactly the opposite. He got good grades in school and knew what he wanted to do with his life. You'd be hard-pressed to find a man more responsible." She sighed heavily. "He's got this sensible, pragmatic way about him. Come to think of it, Evie, you and Scott are a lot alike."

Evie's heart filled up and flowed over. But she wasn't sure if their similarities were pulling them together or pushing them apart. He had offered her everything and Evie had refused him…rejected him…and still he loved her.

And I'm terrified of losing him.

But her logic made no sense. By rejecting Scott she didn't have him…so how could she lose something she didn't have?

Her eyes filled with tears and it took barely seconds for Callie to wrap her arms around Evie's shoulders. "I don't know what to do…what to think. As hard as I've tried not to be, part of me has been so dishonest with him, with *us*."

"There is an *us*?" Callie asked. "I mean is there a you and Scott?"

Evie shrugged, and then nodded. "I'm such an idiot," she admitted.

"Just a woman in love by the look of things."

Evie hiccupped. "Do you mind?"

"About you and Scott? Of course not—he's my brother, you're my friend, I'm married to your brother—it kind of makes us closer than regular sister-in-laws." Callie squeezed her shoulders. "But I think he's in pretty bad shape about this."

Evie knew it and it tore her up inside. "Do you think he still wants to marry me?"

Callie nodded. "But do you want to marry him?"

She shrugged. "His job…"

"His job isn't his life, Evie," Callie said kindly, looking at her stomach, and Evie sensed immediately that her friend knew her fears. "Not anymore. But there's no denying he's good at it. He has two commendations for bravery in the line of duty, was promoted through the ranks well before most people his age and he's always seemed to simply take it all in his stride. Even when his friend died he held it together. He's not a risk, Evie…."

Evie sucked in a quick breath. "But his job is risky," she implored. "And if something happened I'd—"

"We all die, Evie," Fiona said, quieter than usual. "It's how we live that counts."

With those few words it was as though a wave of clarity washed over her and Evie sat, too stunned to move. So many memories surged up and rocked her reality—memories of Gordon and the knowledge that with so many years of grief snapping at her heels, she'd forgotten how it felt to be loved…and to truly live. Occasionally she recalled snapshots of things she'd shared with her husband, like the birth of their son. But the everyday stuff—the often mundane, day-to-day things were the moments that made up a real life. The burnt toast in the morning, the laughter over a shared movie on television, the comfort of strong arms around her as she slept. That was the *living* Fiona spoke of.

And now a genuinely good, honest man wanted to share those things with her.

And I turned him down?

Evie wondered if they made bigger fools than her. "Do...do you really think he'll still want me?"

Callie smiled broadly and hugged her. "Why don't you ask him and find out?"

Fiona laughed and they had all lifted their coffee mugs to clink them together when Callie's cell buzzed. It was obvious the call was from her husband because a dreamy look crossed her face. The look lasted only seconds, though, and when she disconnected Evie knew something was wrong.

"There's trouble down at the surf club," Callie said quickly. "Noah said Trevor was there and you should sit tight and not worry."

Trevor? Trouble? Not worry? Not likely! Evie jerked to her feet. "Trevor's at Cody's on a sleepover."

"Apparently he's not," Callie said. "Cameron and Scott are dealing with it."

Evie's blood ran cold. "I have to get down there."

Callie grabbed her arm. "Noah said you should stay here and he'll call the minute he knows—"

"I'm going," Evie said firmly.

Callie's grip tightened. "Well, I'm coming with you."

Fiona stood. "You both go. I'll stay here with the kids."

Evie was by the door in seconds and her sister-in-law followed closely on her heels.

With scaffolding as the only access point while the building was still undergoing renovations, Scott followed Cameron and they climbed up the outside to investigate.

There were two groups of boys embroiled in a standoff on the top floor of the surf club—one group was clinging to their laptops and backed into a corner, the other group was fueled with aggression while the ringleader held a crudely assembled Molotov cocktail. There didn't appear to be any other weapons involved, but Cameron still approached the scene as dangerous and Scott respected his experience enough to allow him the lead.

Through the dirty window Scott saw Trevor and another boy out in front of their group of friends. They were talking and it looked as though they were trying to reason with the leader of the other group. Scott got a bad vibe from the teenager then and his instinct kicked in immediately. The handmade device in his hand looked lethal enough to do some serious damage, and with the renovations upstairs at the painting stage, there were plenty of combustible materials available if the troubled teen decided to use his weapon.

Scott knew that surprising the boys would only fuel the tension, and followed Cameron back down.

"I'm calling for backup," Cameron said once they hit the ground. He pulled his cell from his pocket and made a call. "They're ten minutes away. I know that kid pretty well," Cameron said. "The one who's holding the weapon is likely to start something once I go in there—he's got a lot of anger issues. Wait outside until the unit gets here."

As much as he wanted to haul Trevor's skinny butt out of there, Scott knew he had to do as Cameron said. If the rules weren't followed, someone might get hurt, and the idea of that someone being Evie's son was unthinkable.

If something happened to Trevor, Evie would be inconsolable. Fear pitched inside his gut, and a deep swell of feeling swept through him. He cared deeply for Evie's son and had an instinctive need to protect him.

He thought about Mike O'Shea, faced with the idea of losing his child, and Scott remembered his friend's frantic rush to race into the house without consideration for the consequences. A father not thinking clearly—a man obsessed with saving his child... Scott had labeled Mike over and over.

I'm going in there. I will do whatever it takes to save

Evie's son. But he knew, without a doubt, that he could do it and still minimize the risks for everyone around him.

I won't lose my head...that's not me. I'm not Mike. I can do both.

A silver utility pulled up about fifty meters away.

When Evie and Callie jumped out and headed toward them, Scott's heart jumped inside his chest.

She launched at Cameron. "Where's my son?"

"Upstairs."

"I'm going up to get him."

"You're doing no such thing," Scott said, and took hold of her arm. "Let Cameron handle this."

She looked at him, all eyes, all fear. "If my son is in danger I'm not going to sit back and—"

"You won't be doing him any favors by charging up there," he said, and quickly explained about the homemade weapon. "The police backup will be here soon. They can diffuse this before it gets out of control."

"But he needs—"

"He needs you to stay calm," Scott said, and tightened his hold on her arm. She looked terrified and he was just about to pull her closer when a stream of loud shouts came from the building, followed by footsteps on bare boards and the unmistakable roar of a fireball breathing into life.

Scott released Evie and raced toward the building, barking out instructions to Cameron to keep everyone back as he moved to scale the scaffolding as quickly as possible. When he reached the top he immediately saw the orange glow of flames through a closed window and heard boys running toward the door. They raced across the threshold in a frightened group, pushing and fighting each other to get through.

He was by the door in a second and instructed the boys to stay calm and file out one at a time. Through the doorway he could see the flames kicking into life, igniting painter's drop sheets.

"Scott!"

Trevor's shaky voice echoed in his ears and he grabbed the boy by the shoulders as he came through the door and hovered, clutching his computer. "Get out now," Scott told him.

"Cody," Trevor said loudly to be heard above the formidable rush of flames. "Cody's stuck in there—he won't come out."

Once the last of the boys were through the door, Scott stepped over the threshold. "You go," he demanded to Trevor. "I'll get him out." Evie's son hesitated and Scott pushed against his chest. "Do what I tell you. Go!"

When Trevor finally turned on his heel, Scott moved into the long room. The flames were running along one wall, igniting the sheets on the floor. He covered his mouth with his forearm and headed across the floorboards. In the distance he heard sirens, and relief pitched behinds his ribs.

He saw the kid backed into the corner, clearly in shock. The flames were closing in on the boy, and Scott skidded across the floor. As he got closer, the fire changed direction, skirting the walls as it hissed and ran around in an arc, combusting a pile of old rags on the floor before it moved dangerously close to the terrified kid.

"Cody," he shouted. "Move to your right and take a couple of big steps."

The teenager coughed and remained where he was as Scott moved closer. The heat pushed him back momentarily and he heard the fire truck pull up outside. But he couldn't wait for backup. The whole room would be engulfed soon. He *had* to get Cody out. There was no time to waste.

He darted to his left, flipping across a low line of fire

that snapped at his heels. The heat smothered his skin and filled his lungs. When he reached Cody, the boy almost fell into his arms.

"Come on, kid," he said as he hauled him over one shoulder. "Let's go."

Evie saw Trevor and rushed forward, oblivious of the fire brigade telling her to stay back. The fire crew worked their way up the building and helped the scared teenagers down the scaffolding.

As soon as she felt her son in her arms, Evie held on to him tightly. "You scared me, Trevor."

"I'm okay," he insisted. "But Cody…Cody's still inside," Trevor said shakily. "Scott told me to get out. He said he'd get Cody down. But he wouldn't move. As soon as the fire started I yelled to everyone to run…but Cody…he wouldn't listen…he wouldn't…he just wouldn't…"

A sob racked her son's thin frame, and Evie hugged him close. Over his shoulder she looked up at the building. Thick smoke billowed from the top floor, and her heart thumped.

Beside her, Evie felt Callie's terror and while she clutched Trevor with one hand, Evie laid her other palm over her stomach. The moments ticked over, every one seeming longer than the one before. And then she saw Scott, illuminated by the beam of torches from the fire-fighters and the bright shadow of the flames behind him. He carried Cody over his shoulder and strode along the scaffolding without missing a step. Three firefighters waited until he'd passed before heading inside the building.

He got to the ground and moved a safe distance away from the building before letting go of Cody. The paramedics were on hand and laid the boy in an awaiting stretcher. By now news of the drama had spread throughout the community and there were people everywhere. The police had now cordoned off around the building, and Evie was held back behind a tape.

Evie heard Noah mutter a relieved "Thank God," and without thinking, she ducked underneath the tape and raced toward Scott.

He looked stunned to see her moving so fast and took a few steps to meet her near the front off the ambulance. "Evie, you shouldn't be run—"

She clutched his shirt, hauled herself against him and kissed him on the mouth. A kiss to stamp herself as his. "You're okay," she breathed, and felt hot tears in her eyes as their lips parted.

He nodded, smiling. "I'm okay."

And with that one look, Evie knew what she wanted. Because she saw…*love.*

"Thank you for getting Trevor out so quickly," she said, clutching his arm. From the light beaming from inside the ambulance she got a good look at him. He had a black smudge on his face, and his T-shirt was scorched near the sleeve. "And for saving Cody."

"It's my—"

"Your job," she said, cutting him off, and smiled. "Yes, I know. I'm glad you were here."

He looked at her oddly. "You're sure about that?"

"Positive."

Someone called his name and he turned away for a moment. Cameron and another police officer were making their way toward them. "I need to talk to these guys," he said, and touched her face. "Why don't you take Trevor home and I'll come by when I'm done?"

Evie didn't want to let him go. "But—"

"Go," he insisted. "I have to make a statement, and they

might want to talk with Trevor later. I'll see you at home." He kissed her forehead and stepped back.

Home... The home she wanted to share with him as they raised their child together.

He turned away to join Cameron just as Evie said his name. He half turned back toward her. "What is it?"

And in that moment Evie gave up her heart. "I love you, Scott."

He let out a ragged breath and stared at her, looking like a man who'd just received the most precious gift in the world. Whatever he was about to say didn't come out because Cameron came up beside him and quickly introduced his colleague. He had business to finish and she needed to give him time to do it. And she was okay with that.

Evie gave Scott one last look before she swiveled on her heel and returned to her son.

When Scott arrived at Dunn Inn, it was close to ten o'clock. Evie had the door open before he'd pulled himself out of his rental car.

When he reached her she didn't say a word and Scott simply took her hand and followed her up the stairs and into the big bedroom at the end of the hall. It was exactly what he expected—pure Evie—there was a soft printed cover on the bed, silky oak furniture and fresh flowers on the armoire near the window.

She shut the door behind them and walked into the middle of the room.

"It's nice in here," he said quietly.

"I should have invited you in here a long time ago," she said quietly as she released his hand. "I'm sorry. I wasn't consciously keeping it off-limits. But I've been alone for so long...I shut off part of myself and in here..." Her arms swept over their surroundings. "In here I could simply be me. The closed-off me who was angry at the world but was too reasonable and sensible to show it."

She took a couple of steps and sat on the padded trunk at the end of the bed. "I had it redecorated after Gordon died. I painted the walls and hung new curtains and picked an outrageously girly bedspread. I guess I was happy in my misery, you know. And then one day you walked through that gate at the airport and smiled at me…and I knew I wasn't as happy in my misery as I'd made out."

Scott's chest tightened. He loved this woman so much. "And now?"

"Now I want…I want to take the life we could have together. The life you offered me."

He took an unsteady step toward her, wanting to fold her in his arms and hold her close. But they needed to talk first, and he needed to be sure. "I have to know something, Evie. Tonight you said you loved me…." Scott swallowed the emotion clutching at his throat. "Was that really about *me?*" he asked.

"I don't understand."

"I mean that sometimes in extreme situations, when a person is pumped on adrenaline and he thinks someone he loves is in danger, the mind can make him think something even if it's not real." He came beside her and sat on the trunk. "Your son was in danger and this feeling you have could just be a kind of misplaced gratitude."

He hated saying it, hated thinking it. But he had to know. Scott had seen it before—he'd seen the victims of accidents cling to their rescuer as if they were a lifeline. If she was only feeling appreciation and relief then he wanted her to tell him so.

And if it's only gratitude, will I take it? Will it be enough?

"Of course I'm grateful," she said, and his heart

thumped inside his chest. "How could I not be?" She grabbed his hand and lifted his knuckles to her mouth, kissing him softly. "You saved my son's life. You saved *all* those boys tonight."

"It's my job, Evie," he said quietly, feeling the meaning in the words more than he'd ever felt them before. "Whether I do it in L.A., or here…it's what I do."

She clutched his hand tightly and Scott felt the connection through to his blood. "I know. I've always known. Tonight I realized something…and I don't just mean because of the fire and saving those kids. I was here with your sister and Fiona and they said something to me that made me realize that perhaps I was wrong to imagine you'd be the kind of man who'd do something risky without thinking of the consequences."

"Not intentionally, no."

"And that's really all I can ask of you," she said softly. "I thought that I wanted you to stop being a firefighter and do something without risks."

Scott's heart settled behind his ribs. "There are no guarantees, Evie."

"I know that, too," she said. "I know what you do can be dangerous and there's no way you can ever be sure you won't get hurt…or worse. But I don't need guarantees, Scott."

"You did," he reminded her.

"I was scared," she admitted. "Scared that I'd lose you, I guess. Scared that I'd have to raise another child alone." She touched his face. "But tonight, I didn't see a man who took chances. I saw a man who was completely in control the whole time, who knew my son was in that building and still did what he had to do. Someone who kept people safe. And that…and that made *me* feel safe."

Scott grabbed her hands and held them against his chest.

"I'll always keep you safe, Evie. You and Trevor and..."
He looked at her slightly swollen belly. "And our baby. I'd
protect you all with my life."

Tears filled her eyes. "I know you would. And I love
you with all my heart."

He kissed her softly and let emotion rise between them.
She grabbed on to his shoulders and clung to him, kissing
him back so hotly, so lovingly, Scott knew he'd never feel
as connected to another soul as he did to this incredible
woman who'd given him her heart and love.

"Just one thing," he said in between kisses. "I realized
something myself tonight—I've been hanging on to this
idea that I couldn't have both—that it needed to be the
job, or a life with someone. But I knew when I was going
into that building that I wasn't like Mike. I was like myself and I *can* do both, Evie. If you ever feel differently
about this—if you're ever worried or want me to stop and
find another type of job to do, promise me you'll tell me."

"I will," she said. "But you know what, I fell in love
with you exactly as you are, exactly who you are. Young,
gorgeous, fearless." She grinned. "That's what I thought
that first day and I still think it now."

"So you're over your worries about the age difference?"

Evie pushed herself against him and smiled. "Ha—I
figure I'll just be thought of as the luckiest woman on the
planet." She touched his cheek. "Anyway, you wait until
you've had months of night feeding and changing dia-
pers—you'll have aged ten years by the time this baby is
a toddler."

"I can't wait," he said honestly.

And it was true. The thought of raising a child with Evie
filled him with such an overwhelming feeling of joy he
could feel the power of it over his skin, through his blood,
in the deep recess of his soul.

"We have to pick out names," she suggested. "I was thinking William for a boy."

Scott nodded. "I like that. It's a good, strong-sounding name."

"And Rebecca for a girl." She kissed him again, lightly along his jaw, and whispered against his ear. "Rebecca Jones."

Scott pulled back slightly. "Jones?"

Evie smiled. "Mmm," she breathed against his skin.

"But you turned me—"

"I'm an idiot," she said, and slipped to the floor in front of him. She perched herself between his knees. "Would you mind if I asked you instead?"

Mind? He couldn't believe what he was hearing. The woman he loved, the woman carrying his child was about to ask him the most important question in the world. Scott shook his head. "Not at all."

She took a deep breath, grabbed his hands and held them against her breasts. "Scott, would you marry me?"

"Absolutely." He kissed her, thinking it was the best moment of his life. "I love you, Evie."

"And I love you. Always. Forever." She ran her hands over his shoulders and across his chest, plucking at the smudgy marks on the fabric. "You're a mess," she said as she wiped her fingertips along his cheek. "So how about that spa bath I promised you a while back?"

Scott looked toward the beckoning ensuite bathroom. "Lead the way."

She smiled and stood, taking his hands. "How about we go together?"

Now that was *definitely* the best moment in his life.

Epilogue

Evie loved Christmas. Especially this year. The big tree in the living room sparkled with colored lights and dozens of glass ornaments and there were so many gifts underneath she couldn't stop grinning when she imagined the room come morning and how all that wrapping paper would be strewn across the floor.

"I do think this year the tree is the best it's ever looked."

Evie turned as Flora Manning came into the room. "Yes," Evie agreed. "It's all those extra lights."

Flora raised a silvery brow. "That's not it," she said, and fiddled with a stray green frond. "It's you."

"Me?"

"You're happy," Flora explained. "Happier than I've ever seen. That's why this big tree looks so special."

Evie smiled. She *was* happy. She had everything she'd ever asked for and more—a wonderful son, an adorable baby and a husband she loved with all her heart. The tree was a bonus. And as it was their first Christmas as a complete family, Evie could barely contain her excitement. They would open some gifts tonight with her mother-in-law and the Manning sisters and tomorrow her parents were coming over to share the morning festivities with them. Later they would all go to Noah and Callie's for a family celebration.

This time of year would always be special to her. She'd fallen in love with Scott during Christmas twelve months earlier and those memories were etched deep within her heart. They'd shared gifts around the tree and kissed beneath the mistletoe and this year would be the same. Only now, Scott was her husband and the tree and the plastic mistletoe had more meaning for her than ever before.

Once Flora left the room to find her sister, Evie spent a little more time trimming the tree and rearranging the gifts. She'd prepared her usual punch and fruit cake and had a tray of savories warming in the oven for later. A soft and familiar sound caught her attention and she turned around.

Her husband framed the doorway, holding their precious bundle in his arms.

"She's supposed to be asleep," Evie said gently, and walked across the room. Scott held their three-month-old daughter, Rebecca, against his shoulder as she pumped her chubby legs excitedly. Evie touched the baby's soft hair. "She'll be relentless tomorrow if she doesn't sleep tonight."

Scott smiled and kissed his daughter's head. "She was awake in her crib, talking to herself. I think she said Dada again."

Evie's brows slanted upward. "You know she's too young to speak, right?"

"Not my kid," he said proudly, and cradled her head with his hand. "She's advanced for her age."

Evie knew there was little point insisting otherwise. "Yes, darling, of course she is."

Scott grinned. "And she loves the Christmas tree lights," he said, and waited while Evie flicked the switch and the tree illuminated in a kaleidoscope of flickering color. Rebecca's blue eyes widened and she gurgled delightfully. "See?" Scott said, and smiled.

Evie watched her daughter and husband together and a surge of love rushed through her blood. He was such an incredible father to both the baby and Trevor. They'd been married for six months, and each day had been an incredible joy. Scott had joined the Bellandale Fire and Rescue Department and had settled easily into his new job.

Trevor loped through the doorway, looking very grown up at sixteen. "Are we opening presents?" he asked, and grabbed some cake.

"Soon," Evie promised as the Manning sisters came through the door. "Once everyone is settled."

Scott winked at her. They'd bought Trevor a fancy racing bike to go with his newfound interest in fitness and sports. The gift was hidden in the one vacant downstairs bedroom, and both she and Scott excused themselves at the same time so they could bring it into the living room.

"I'll take the baby," Eleanor insisted as she floated into the room wearing one of her signature silk caftans. Scott's mother had become a regular visitor to Crystal Point over the past year. One day, Evie was sure, it would become a permanent move. Especially if they continued to add to their brood. She loved the idea of having another child in a year or so.

As Scott placed Rebecca in his mother's arms, Amelia and Flora starting laughing.

"Look, mistletoe!"

Evie tilted her neck backward. Sure enough, the green-

ry was hanging from the door frame above. She looked
t Scott and smiled, thinking how it was such a perfect
moment. "Have you been decorating again?"

He chuckled and drew her against his solid body. "Who?
Me?" he said, and kissed her under the mistletoe before he
eached up and twirled the leaves with his fingertips. "You
know, I owe a lot to this little piece of plastic."

"You do?"

"Sure. You might say it's the reason we're here. Got you
o kiss me, didn't it?"

Evie laughed delightfully. "Or got *you* to kiss *me?*"

He looked into her eyes. "It got us both here—and that's
ll that matters."

She nodded and smiled. It was, for sure, the best Christmas ever.

* * * *

Don't miss Helen Lacey's next book,
HIS-AND-HERS FAMILY
On sale January 2013
wherever Harlequin books are sold!

REQUEST YOUR FREE BOOKS!
2 FREE NOVELS PLUS 2 FREE GIFTS!

♣ Harlequin®

SPECIAL EDITION
Life, Love & Family

YES! Please send me 2 FREE Harlequin® Special Edition novels and my 2 FREE gifts (gifts are worth about $10). After receiving them, if I don't wish to receive any more books, I can return the shipping statement marked "cancel." If I don't cancel, I will receive 6 brand-new novels every month and be billed just $4.49 per book in the U.S. or $5.24 per book in Canada. That's a saving of at least 14% off the cover price! It's quite a bargain! Shipping and handling is just 50¢ per book in the U.S. and 75¢ per book in Canada.* I understand that accepting the 2 free books and gifts places me under no obligation to buy anything. I can always return a shipment and cancel at any time. Even if I never buy another book, the two free books and gifts are mine to keep forever.

235/335 HDN FEGF

Name _____ (PLEASE PRINT)

Address _____ Apt. #

City _____ State/Prov. _____ Zip/Postal Code

Signature (if under 18, a parent or guardian must sign)

Mail to the **Reader Service:**
IN U.S.A.: P.O. Box 1867, Buffalo, NY 14240-1867
IN CANADA: P.O. Box 609, Fort Erie, Ontario L2A 5X3

Not valid for current subscribers to Harlequin Special Edition books.

Want to try two free books from another line?
Call 1-800-873-8635 or visit www.ReaderService.com.

* Terms and prices subject to change without notice. Prices do not include applicable taxes. Sales tax applicable in N.Y. Canadian residents will be charged applicable taxes. Offer not valid in Quebec. This offer is limited to one order per household. All orders subject to credit approval. Credit or debit balances in a customer's account(s) may be offset by any other outstanding balance owed by or to the customer. Please allow 4 to 6 weeks for delivery. Offer available while quantities last.

Your Privacy—The Reader Service is committed to protecting your privacy. Our Privacy Policy is available online at www.ReaderService.com or upon request from the Reader Service.

We make a portion of our mailing list available to reputable third parties that offer products we believe may interest you. If you prefer that we not exchange your name with third parties, or if you wish to clarify or modify your communication preferences, please visit us at www.ReaderService.com/consumerschoice or write to us at Reader Service Preference Service, P.O. Box 9062, Buffalo, NY 14269. Include your complete name and address.

HSE11B

The Bowman siblings have avoided Christmas ever since a family tragedy took the lives of their parents during the holiday years ago. But twins Trace and Taft Bowman have gotten past their grief, courtesy of the new women in their lives. Is it sister Caidy's turn to find love—perhaps with the new veterinarian in town?

Read on for an excerpt from
A COLD CREEK NOEL by USA TODAY
bestselling author RaeAnne Thayne, next in her
ongoing series THE COWBOYS OF COLD CREEK

***

"For what it's worth, I think the guys around here are crazy. Even if you did grow up with them."

He might have left things at that, safe and uncomplicated, except his eyes suddenly shifted to her mouth and he didn't miss the flare of heat in her gaze. He swore under his breath, already regretting what he seemed to have no power to resist, and then he reached for her.

As his mouth settled over hers, warm and firm and tasting of cocoa, Caidy couldn't quite believe this was happening.

She was being kissed by the sexy new veterinarian, just a day after thinking him rude and abrasive. For a long moment she was shocked into immobility, then heat began to seep through her frozen stupor. Oh. Oh, yes!

How long had it been since she had enjoyed a kiss and wanted more? She was astounded to realize she couldn't really remember. As his lips played over hers, she shifted her neck slightly for a better angle. Her insides seemed to give a collective shiver. Mmm. This was exactly what two people ought to be doing at 3:00 a.m. on a cold December day.

He made a low sound in his throat that danced down her spine, and she felt the hard strength of his arms slide around her, pulling her closer. In this moment, nothing else seemed to matter but Ben Caldwell and the wondrous sensations fluttering through her.

Still, this was crazy. Some tiny voice of self-preservation seemed to whisper through her. What was she doing? She had no business kissing someone she barely knew and wasn't even sure she liked yet.

Though it took every last ounce of strength, she managed to slide away from all that delicious heat and move a few inches away from him, trying desperately to catch her breath.

The distance she created between them seemed to drag Ben back to his senses. He stared at her, his eyes looking as dazed as she felt. "That was wrong. I don't know what I was thinking. Your dog is a patient and…I shouldn't have…"

She might have been offended by the dismay in his voice if not for the arousal in his eyes. But his hair was a little rumpled and he had the evening shadow of a beard and all she could think was *yum*.

***

Can Caidy and Ben put their collective pasts behind them and find a brilliant future together?

Find out in A COLD CREEK NOEL, coming in December 2012 from Harlequin Special Edition. And coming in 2013, also from Harlequin Special Edition, look for Ridge's story….

When legacy commands, these Greek royals must obey!

Discover a page-turning new Harlequin Presents®
duet from *USA TODAY* bestselling author

Maisey Yates

A ROYAL WORLD APART

Desperate to escape an arranged marriage, Princess
Evangelina has tried every trick in her little black book
to dodge her security guards. But where everyone else
has failed, will her new bodyguard bend her to his
will...and steal her heart?

Available November 13, 2012.

AT HIS MAJESTY'S REQUEST

Prince Stavros Drakos rules his country like his
business—with a will of iron! And when duty demands
an heir, this resolute bachelor will turn his sole
focus to the task....

But will he finally have met his match in a world-
renowned matchmaker?

**Coming December 18, 2012,
wherever books are sold.**

Harlequin® *Desire*

ALWAYS POWERFUL, PASSIONATE AND PROVOCATIVE.

DON'T MISS THE SEDUCTIVE CONCLUSION TO THE MINISERIES

THE HIGHEST BIDDER

WITH FAN-FAVORITE AUTHOR

BARBARA DUNLOP

Prince Raif Khouri believes that Waverly's
high-end-auction-house executive Ann Richardson
is responsible for the theft of his valuable antique Gold
Heart statue, rumored to be a good luck charm to his
family. The only way Raif can keep an eye on her—
and get the truth from her—is by kidnapping Ann and
taking her to his kingdom. But soon Raif finds himself
the prisoner as Ann tempts him like no one else.

A GOLDEN BETRAYAL

Available December 2012 from Harlequin® Desire.